A Thousand Hearts

Gordon Dangerfield

ISBN: 978-1-9161174-0-2

This book is dedicated, with love and gratitude, to the memory of my mum, Nancy Dangerfield

Why should I speak of what a thousand hearts
Have felt, and every man alive can guess?

-- William Wordsworth, *The Prelude*

1

The grey water so cold that the rubber in your wetsuit flapped empty already in the place where your balls used to be, the surprising taste of the salt, and the oddness of the surprise, you'd been to the beach enough times to know fine well that the water would be salty. Andy flattened himself on the gently lurching board and thrust an arm down on each side as far as he could stretch, churning through the gathering wave, tasting the salt again, and knowing suddenly that the picture was to blame for the surprise, that it was because everything in the picture was so clear and clean and sunny and blue that it chased all the coldness and greyness and salt right out of your thinking. It was the picture, and it was the Classic Grand, duping you like a bogus milk boy, lying in wait for you with a surf flick when all you went there for was porn.

Smiling a bit to think of it, jaw clenched and teeth chittering, the team wades to the pictures, the Rio first and The Warriors, Waldo up and down on his seat like a demented three year old, announcing to the whole cinema that the seats were bouncy, and then the film carrying all of you right along with it, bumping shoulders as you walked out up the aisle, grunting and swaggering, only half kidding, and in the car Nate doing the voice, Warr-ee-ors come out to play-ee, and rattling his keys off the Irn Bru bottle, the dead spit of the guy and funny as the wolf, and Joe, quite serious, how if you got the Twechar boys and the Kilsyth boys and the Bishopbriggs boys, you could take over Kirkie, and all of you cracking up all over again, what the fuck would you do with Kirkie if you had it. Then the Rio again and The Kentucky Fried Movie, a couple of funny bits, the game show with Hung Well and Long Wang, and please welcome our third contestant Enormous Genitals, the Joy of Sex album with the solution for premature ejaculation, supplied free, and Big Jim Slade bursts in and carries off the wee guy's woman, and then the next week Mack looking over his pint in the Vale, there's a triple bill in the Classic Grand the night, and he could hardly get the names out for laughing, Boys and Girls Get Together, Behind Convent Walls, Mary Millington's True Blue Confessions.

And you laughed too but you had the horn a wee bit at the thought of it just the same, and into your mind Nate reading aloud from Climax magazine while the rest of you hooted, such was the force of his lustful passion as the guy got a blowjob under his coat, and Nate admitting later that the thing had given him a semi but still not abashed really, why should he be when he was hung like a horse and even the graffiti in the school bogs paid tribute to the fact, and it wasn't long before he was just making it up as he went along, unless Climax magazine really did have Joseph of Arimathea getting a handjob from the Ezekiel that month, and the whole crowd around marvelling at this Coming of the Lord.

And everyone round the table in the Vale must have been the same because you all laughed plenty at the names and at the neck of turning up in full public view at the Classic Grand, but when Mack said he would take care of getting the tickets as long as he got everyone's money in advance you all said you were in quickly enough, and Nora too, you'd talked her into it she said. Then the five of you crammed into the creaky wee wreck of a lift and apparently the doorman guy had to come too, the thing taking about a million years to get up to the top, and there was no point in looking at the numbers, all it had was a nothing and a one, and you could hardly look at one another or even worse at the doorman guy for fear of cracking up, whether from hilarity or fear you didn't even know. The single guys dotted around in the darkness and casting quick hysterical looks at each other when the branch fell out of the sky and the young nympho nun, you must have missed what she was doing in the convent, smiled up to thank the heavens and then carved the branch into a dildo, and you were still recovering from that when the celestial music started, and the randy young priest rolled up, and then it wasn't too much later that you were catching each other looking more and more often in Nora's direction, and she just kept looking at the screen and pretending not to notice, but you could tell she wasn't unhappy about all the attention, and once you caught her having a sly look herself over at Mack, and he saw her and smiled back, the smile he had that was sleekit as fuck and strangely guileless and innocent at the same time.

Surprise, surprise, Mack all quiet on the drive home, you could hear the gears grinding in his crafty wee brain, see him working out how he could drop everyone else off before Nora and make it look as natural as possible, and he knew that you knew, and you knew that he knew you knew, and Nate giving a sarcastic commentary on the points of interest along these scenic new routes you were taking, and Nora riding shotgun and saying nothing, and you wondered what she was thinking, if she'd got the horn too at what had been on the screen or if she was just pleased to be getting her chance with Mack. Then the very next night in the Vale, red neck and no denying it, but Mack as usual laughing as much as the rest of you at the debacle of it, the drive up to Drumshanty Woods and getting off with Nora, everything going fine until he hears the bunch of wee boys round the Yellow Banana Bendy Buggy, ya dirty old bastard, and still a whole night later he has no idea why they thought he was old, but him and Nora have to get themselves adjusted and get the Bendy Buggy the fuck out of there as quick as they can, and that's the end of that, and serves him right anyway for being such a sleekit bastard according to Nate, the cunt would ride your sister.

Then the second and, up to now, last time to the Classic Grand, same team, Mack said, veterans only, except Nate was crying off the pictures for a bit after the Odeon debacle, so it was just you, Allie and Mack and big wow, Nora was up for it again and this time she didn't even pretend she wasn't. The Odeon debacle still all too fresh in your own mind too, a half day at your work and meeting Nate after his exam in the morning, the poor guy Stephen that never had more than a pint before in his life tagging along, five pints each in the Muscular Arms in about an hour or something, and then someone's bright idea of the pictures, The Pink Panther Strikes Again, and the guy Stephen in fits of laughter at some random thing like hello, and then you throwing up into your Wrangler jacket right there in your seat, the two wee old dears in front of you not even turning round, they must have been too mortified or maybe just too polite to say anything, and Nate best of all, making it out into the lobby, throwing up in his hand, thinking about it for a second and then tossing it casually over his shoulder, and carrying on to the bogs. Telling the manager that him and the guy Stephen had just failed an exam, they'd had a few pies and a few pints, and the manager giving him his money back but not you or Stephen, you weren't being asked to leave, even though you were both in much worse shape than the big man was, as the two wee old dears could have told him just from the reek of puke and all the hughying noises going on behind them, and you could see Nate's point, you wanted to scream with embarrassment yourself when you thought of it, but Mack was right too, you had to see the funny side.

And then jackpot, there's no porn at the Classic Grand on a Tuesday, it's a licensing thing the guy says, and they have to show a real film, and it's Big Wednesday, some beach blanket movie that you can't even remember from the real pictures, and Mack and Nora are up for it of course and Allie is up for anything, the amenable bastard, and the film as bogus as you knew it would be, Mack and Nora tampering surreptitiously with each other on one side of you and Allie chewing gum in your ear on the other, but then the surfers actually get in the water and it's unbelievable, you can't take your eyes off the screen, and so you hold on and hold on for Big Wednesday, you know it has to be coming, and when it does it's the most exhilarating thing you ever saw in your life, the speed and the skill and the danger, and something much deeper, you don't even know, and even the terrible corniness of it makes a kind of sense now, it's a test of a surfer to ride alone, you shouldn't have to depend on anyone but yourself, the slow motion shots right inside the huge wave, terrifying and wonderful, and the wipeouts, tumbling and tumbling, and no reason to think you would ever see the surface again, tumbling and tumbling forever in a deep blue world, mystical and beautiful and strange.

No point in trying to talk to the rest of them, they're oblivious for their own various reasons, and now you're the quiet one on the way home, and it's like something's taken over you, and there's a path all lit up in front of you and there's nothing to do but go down it. And looking back now at the beach, still quite close and disappointing really, you thought you'd paddled further, but anyway you were outside at least, beyond the point where the sullen waves were breaking, you could see the next set off in the distance, dark and dangerous-looking, but you've come this far, just concentrate on what you have to do, make sure you've gauged the lineup right and take your bearings for later from two points on the shore, and okay, look for your wave, that one, paddle like fuck and spring your feet up onto the board as you feel it moving underneath you. Okay. Now.

It felt amazing, standing upright, held up there in all the energy of the universe, and maybe it lasted only a few seconds but it could have been a million years, and a million things in your mind at once, and still you knew somehow as it was happening that they were really all the same thing, that there was some dark invisible workmanship pulling on all the elements at odds with each other inside you, making them move together for just this moment as one, as if by miraculous gift, shaking off the burden of your own unnatural self, surprising suddenly in your vital soul a fierce desire to be worthy of yourself.

Then quickly the wipeout, a wee baby one, a neck to even call it that in a few feet of water above soft sand, the gentle surf carrying you in and your board waiting for you in the fizzing white foam on the beach, and now you weren't even feeling the cold, seeing the greyness, tasting the salt. You didn't know how, but you'd been right that night to see what you saw, and now the prospect open before you at last of purposeful activity, of future prowess in an honourable field, something holy nearly, and yet almost an injury to think of anything in this moment but the present joy of it, to enslave the precious liberty of it with any hopes or expectations.

Andy turned his board back round into the gently breaking surf and started to paddle out again to the lineup.

2

There had been other things before Big Wednesday but none of them had lasted and none of them had been enough. You thought hard about it, and maybe that was part of the problem, thinking too hard, and thinking too much, and you thought yourself right into a corner, and in the end nothing you could do about any of it anyway. There was your family, you loved them and you knew they loved you, and you wished you could do what you knew they wanted for you, but for some reason you couldn't, and there was your mates, and that was it, you had a vague uneasy feeling that you were missing something, but you couldn't seem to ever work out quite what it was. All you knew was all the things you were supposed to care about and didn't, education and work and politics and making something of yourself, you looked around at the people who were doing it, and it didn't fill you with admiration or envy like it was supposed to, but something else instead, contempt was the closest to it probably, except that it was sad and shallow and empty, not angry and fulfilling like contempt should be. That was why only the team made any sense, the laughs and the stories, and not giving too much of a fuck about any of it.

Your mum said you were an anarchist, but you knew she was just saying that to be kind, to give you a fancy name that might jildy you up a bit, get you interested in politics or the things her and your dad believed in, or off to Uni like Louise, it wasn't too late if you went to Langside and did your Highers again, you weren't an anarchist, you were something that didn't have a name, someone that didn't want to be told what to do and yet didn't know yourself either. Wishing you could commit to something, want a career like Louise or be a socialist like your mum and dad, not that they would ever join the Labour Party, it was too right wing, but your mum was strong in the union, she still believed in it, you could never see why, always wee fat corpulent guys with big bulbous red drinkers' noses, broken veins in their faces too, and you knew at least one had a steel plate in his head, pontificating in their whisky-soaked voices, fiddling their expenses at conferences, doing fuck all except run around feeling important and kissing management's browner, the last fuckers you'd turn to for help, and the councillors worse, corrupt to the back teeth, and if Thatcher did start selling

Council houses, they'd be at the front of the protest march shouting their heads off, big fat hypocrites, they were the most right wing of the lot, houses for all their relatives and not giving a fuck about anything except the loss of their own power, their own wee private empires.

Nate would roll his eyes at you then, not that you said it exactly like that, I think there's a basic flaw in the comrade's analysis, and your mum and dad didn't mind when he came back to crash on the couch, it was a long walk back to Lenzie when you were half-cut, and they liked Nate because he was mature and understood about politics and was left wing even if he was awful cynical himself for such a young man, and Nate would agree with them about the unions and the need to organize and about Thatcher the milk snatcher and your dad said he'd like to see her work a shift in the yards or go down a mine, she wouldn't last a day, and then she might have some idea of what she was talking about, her heid buttoned up the back, and your mum said yes, she had a rare face for kicking, and Nate, smoking your old man's smeegs, and drinking tea, and telling them about student politics up at the Uni, about the privatization of the services at the QM Union, he'd never join the GUU, it had been men only for centuries and just this year forced to mix, and some bunch called ARA Catering winning the food tender for the dinner hall, and the wee guy standing for the QM Board, someone asked him for his policy on ARA, and he stood up there, proud and defiant and earnest, I fully support the aims and means of the Provisional IRA, and Nate himself had joined the Troops Out Movement, it had to be partly to noise up his old man, and their first speaker got huckled at Stranraer, and then Nate wrapping the blankets and sheets round his big frame on the couch, still snoring away when you came down in the morning and your mum and dad huddled behind the partition, talking quietly so as not to wake him, but you would wake him, glad he was there, grateful to him as you always would be for signing you onto the team.

It wasn't as if you had any time yourself for Thatcher, she seemed to have no kindness in her, no friends even if she thought she had, and no doubt your dad was right about her working a shift in the yards, though in fairness you'd be scared to do it yourself, you had it pretty cushy too, and you thought of your Pop, there wouldn't even be any Thatcher if they were all like him in the union, the postcard, you still had it, in pencil, in his neat careful hand, hello Andy, this is to let you know that the place where I work made these two bridges, I hope you are having good fun with your toys, the pride radiating off it, in the bridges and in you. Walking along the Clyde with him, come on Andy, we'll let these women talk and we'll get away out, the competition to see who could make the fruit pastille last the longest and you had to stick your tongue out to show the wee bit of green goo, and you were thrilled if you won, and the Clyde then, almost level with you on the path, dark and dirty and deep, the black sluggish currents and the foaming chemicals, if you fell in you'd just disappear under it and never be seen again, and strange shapes floating just below the surface, and you felt like a real man too walking along there with your Pop, and the only time you ever saw him angry when you climbed the big chute, and he said are you really sure about this Andy and you said yes I promise I'll go down it Pop, and then you were too scared at the top and the big kids had to pass you down into his arms through the rails, and your Pop silent and brooding for a while, and the relief when he was himself again, and up the close, into the warm kitchen, hoisted on his strong shoulders, laughing wildly, hurrah the funny wee barra's mine, it disnae belang tae O'Hara, the fly wee bloke stuck tae ma roak, so ahm just stickin tae his barra, and would you hold my coat Malone, hold my coat Malone, give a right good cheer and do not fear, for the boys can hold their own, you didn't really know why it was funny but you laughed along with your Pop, still up on his shoulders, it felt great to do it. And sometimes he would talk, when he thought you were asleep on the big recess bed, and you'd listen, half understanding, about James Maxton that told Ramsay MacDonald sit down man, you're a bloody tragedy, your Pop loved Maxton, and your mum too, and your Pop dragging your Grandma to see him at the ILP street meeting and some louts heckling him, God save the King, and your wee Grandma, with never a word to say about politics, beside herself at the bad manners of it, turning round to them, God save the King is it, you folk would cut the King's throat for ten shillings, and your Pop taking her gently by the arm, I think we'll be moving along now Agnes, and he would talk about when your mum was wee in the room and kitchen they had then, and how your Grandma had kept the floorboards spotless when they had no linoleum or carpet, and she could make a pot of soup out of the fat from the mince, and your Pop going round the Barras at the weekends for cheap tools for the apprentices, how could they live on what they were paid, they had to have the chance to be young, and your Grandma, they wouldn't do it for you Sam, and your Pop, that's not the point Agnes, and your Grandma secretly proud of him and fiercely loyal always.

And when he got beat up by some random thugs and he walked home and the whole way no-one offered to help him even though his face was cut and bleeding and even your mum was disgusted and sickened and thought he should be angry at people for once, your Pop just said people are scared to get involved Annie, and your mum said okay, the angry tears still in her eyes, but your Grandma thought different, and from that moment, she always said that the working man wasn't worth fighting for, and all your Pop would do was shake his head and smile, he'd never believe it, but surely it was true, in the end everyone looked after themselves. And then your mum crying, your Pop was dead, a heart attack, and her friend trying to be kind, when you think of it, you're just crying for yourself, and your mum said no, I'm crying for my children too.

And that was how your mum was raised, and your dad not much different, working class and proud of it, and your mum trying to tell you that you were working class too, and maybe she still was, for all she was a speech therapist and your dad a college teacher now, but you weren't, your whole life spent in Rosebank, and your semi-detached Wimpey, lower middle class maybe, but Spam Valley definitely, and most of the rest of them too, maybe not Mack, the Council house in Harestanes and an apprentice now at the foundry, or Joe, working class stamped through him like Blackpool rock, for all he lived out at Shiloh now, and his old man with probably more money than the rest of you put together. It was education, your mum said, and that was your Pop again too, each generation builds on the last, and you keep fighting for your class, it's what they did, and Louise now at the Uni, the first generation to go, and what they wanted for you, and your O grades so good, but then in Fifth Year getting signed onto the team, all interest in following orders quickly gone, the thrill of Joe pulling wheelies in the school car park, and you ran and piled into the brief, and everyone watching, wishing it was them, up the Campsies to the Glencraig in your school shirt and trousers, and the guy there just glad for the business, well scooshed on one pint, or just dogging it at Allie's, I'll put the kettle on if you make the tea, the Pistols and the Clash and the Jam and Allie's endless collection of singles, Wire and The Mekons, Penetration and The Fall, Wreckless Eric and Patrik Fitzgerald and John Cooper Clarke, he had them all before anyone else in Kirkie, picture sleeves and coloured vinyl and all the honours.

And the teachers were decent, most of them, maybe they knew it was all bullshit themselves or they just thought it was your funeral, it wasn't as if you were giving them any major hassle, and whatever, they didn't give you too hard a time, and maybe the association with Mack and Waldo, they lived a charmed life the bastards, Waldo with the Disprin in chemistry, here boys, watch this, and it all foaming up, and Hen Broon running out to get the Head of Department and the two of them taking notes, you're sure you didn't add anything and the three of you swearing you didn't, and then them finding the dregs of it, and big Hen, genuinely raging for a few seconds and then rolling his eyes and giving Waldo a kiddie-on clip round the ear, laughing himself at the brass neck of it, and only a week later loaning Waldo all the tubes and glassware for the still and even taking a swig of the stuff when Waldo brought it in, the wee perfume bottle, more alcohol in the dregs of the perfume probably than the glorified bogwater Waldo produced. And the time when Mack farted, Waldo rolling around, coughing and spluttering, sir, he's rotten sir, put him in the fume cupboard sir, Hen just laughing as usual, but not wee Morrison the time in RME with Mack and Allie and Nate, all of you in stitches and Morrison marching you down to his office, who let air, and you couldn't help but lose it at that, the more you tried to keep it in the worse it got, and finally Mack, we don't know what you mean sir, and Morrison red in the face, right, I was in the army, the Rector was in the army, Mr Taylor was in the army, we know the words, who farted, and that was it, you were all on the floor, and then the belt was out, but it didn't even hurt, everybody knew that Morrison couldn't draw it worth a fuck anyway.

And old Gulliver in history was pretty decent too, Waldo asking him what was the name of that port the Germans bombed sir, and Gulliver, I can't tell you that Derek, this is a test, and Waldo, ach come on, sir, I know what happened and everything, I just can't remember the name, and all hurt that Gulliver wouldn't tell him, or when he asked what organization supplied stuff for the army, come on it begins with a C, and Waldo, Coopers sir, no Derek, the Co-op sir, no Derek, not the Co-op either, and Waldo, when he failed the test, never mind sir, Winston Churchill was a diddy at school, and old Gulliver, Derek, Winston Churchill was a diddy till the day he died. And not just Churchill, the Prefects coming round with the poppies, and Gulliver refusing to buy one, Earl Haig Fund is it, Earl Haig, the Butcher of the Somme, I don't think so, and your mum liked that one and pleased you had at least one good teacher at the place.

And always something with Waldo, setting Brim's hair on fire with the model aeroplane fuel, Brim running round and round the garden and Waldo in fits, or trying to turbo his old man's diesel lawnmower with the hoover, sticking the pole up its rear end and chasing it round the garden himself, cutting the top of an action man's head off, cold porridge for the filling, and then tomato sauce for the body, the holes plugged with plasticine, blasting away with an air pistol, I'm telling you boys, it was brilliant, and now he was a police cadet, some maniac letting him borrow a shotgun, and all proud that he shot a hare, trying to get you to go and see it in the garage, come on and say hello to Hartley boys, say hello to Hartley. And the tales from down the station, right, you're done for a rush breach, and the poor punter, what's a rush breach, and Waldo, a night in the cells for fuck all, the rush of air as he hits the back of the van, and Nate shaking his head, another example of the arbitrary power of the state, it's cunts like you we're fighting against, but he was laughing too, you couldn't help it with Waldo.

You half wondered what they might say at the school if they saw you now, haunting the Mitchell, the Kirkie Library had fuck all about surfing needless to say, poring over the same book night after night till they closed, more grateful than ever for the brief, for passing your driving test first time, and Joe, fuck knows how that happened, and Mack, we've got to get the man on the road, out with the snips in the Evening Times, and can't contain himself when he sees the Viva with an MOT, and he has to phone the guy, are you sure, a Viva with an MOT, and the guy must have known right away he was at it, aye son, I'm sure, it's got an MOT all right, and Mack, a Viva with an MOT, I've got to have it, I've no got any money but I've got these five magic beans, and the guy, well I'm not sure I could let it go for that son, and Mack, I can throw in a wee tartan pencil case, the guy saying he's still not sure, and Mack, you see, it's for the new James Bond movie, Vivas United, but finally he saw one that he actually did think was promising and you went to look at it, a squib of an Escort, and bright turquoise, the worst paint job ever, and worse even than the Bendy Buggy but at least not an Estate, and Joe said what do you expect for fuck all and him and Mack gave it their seal of approval, and sure enough, they had it running in a week, up and down to the scrappie every night and you and Nate making them cups of tea, and holding ropes and handing them tools, you understood fuck all and cared less, but you had to admit, for such brainless bastards, they definitely had a knack for it. The freedom it gave you, running like a burst arse half the time but you didn't care, you could go anywhere any time you wanted, door to door, and the stereo fitted courtesy of Allie the sparkie, it was worth more than the whole rest of the brief put together, the windows open and blasting Graham Parker or maybe Tom Petty, the pure joy of that first album, up all night with his pals and in the morning on the phone to tell his girlfriend's boss he's a jerk, and now five nights running driving out to the Mitchell, gloating over every word in the book, scribbling notes for later, immersed in the world of surfing, somehow you could just always imagine how it might feel, ignoring the bits about tricks and competitions and getting your body in shape, that wasn't what it was about, you knew already, it's a test of a surfer to ride alone, just you and the waves, and that was everything, you just somehow knew it.

And it seemed you couldn't just surf at any old beach, you needed a certain kind of wave, and for all you knew maybe there weren't even any waves like that in Scotland, you couldn't ever remember seeing an actual surfer in the flesh, but there was an address at the back of the book for the British Surfing Federation and when you wrote to them they actually wrote right back, there were waves you could surf on the east coast and up north, and they even gave you the phone number for a guy in Dunallan, and dear Andy, we're very pleased to welcome you to the world of surfing, your life will never be the same again, may you never stop looking for that perfect wave, and the thrill it gave you, you must have read it a thousand times, and couldn't bring yourself to phone the number for days, and then did, Colin McIvor, just call me Duke son, and arranged to meet him at the weekend, just like that.

And that was Colin McIvor, the Duke, an old guy in his fifties somewhere, his hair grey where he wasn't baldy, about as tall as you and not a pick on him, but fit and strong, he reminded you of your Pop for all your Pop was short and stocky, the same energy bouncing off him, you liked him the moment you saw him, and he even seemed to understand when you looked down at your feet and said you didn't really want any lessons, he just smiled, you just want to get out there, don't you Andy, you want to do it for yourself, and you said yes, the gratitude flooding through you, and he had an old wetsuit and boots and a board for you, we can work something out if you take to it, he said, and he smiled again, like he knew he was inducting you into some secret society, and he told you where the main beach was, there was only ever himself and a few others surfing it, he said, but if you take my advice, Andy, you'll look for your own spots, there's plenty out there, your only problem is finding a place to park where you don't have to walk half a mile to where they're breaking, and you knew right there you were going to do just that, and fuck the parking, how hard could it be, and wasn't Mack just after spotting Joe's Mark III parked right in the middle of a field, his big white arse going up and down, and Mack, practically choking on his pint, I like my Nat King as much as the next man, but for fuck's sake, a fucking field, how much of a grunter was she, and Joe, crimson with embarrassment and ready to pap Mack's napper, but still it was true and even he had to just sit there and take it, there was nothing you could do when Mack got something like that on you.

3

Things you never thought you'd do. Andy sat peering at the woman on the telly, trying to study the highs and lows on the map of Europe behind her and listen to her at the same time, and why did they all talk like that, like Radio One deejays, as if all that mattered was filling the space with sound, practically impossible to decipher the actual sense of it and maybe no-one really cared, you never had yourself in all fairness. You thought about Duke and the handful of other surfers you'd met, like ships passing in the night in Duke's garage, they'd all be watching too right now, eager and hopeful, and Duke getting you your very own key cut for the garage, and everyone's boards and gear piled around the place on the dusty concrete floor, it must have been worth a fair amount all told, and you knew that no-one would even think of touching anything, the same look common to all eyes, and Duke showing you what to look for on the telly and the radio, and in the papers, a storm hundreds of miles away good news for the swells in the two or three wee spots you'd found.

Then your body aching all the time at first, you had to find an honourable way to get it fit for the purpose, a way fitted for a thing of such high attempt, switching from the cushy job in the sorting office to bog standard postman, your manager trying to talk you out of it and all the usual mince about promotions and career opportunities, but your mum and dad not bothered at all, it was all a dead end to them anyway, and more money in fact for walking a route, your mum, I'll have an extra couple of pounds dig money then, not that she cared a toss about that either.

Walking as fast as you could in the cold morning air, the bag loaded as heavy as you could get it, and a good sweat on already, so much better than the hot airless office, you wished you'd thought of it before, your route nearly always done by the middle of the morning, and the same in the afternoon, time on your hands and you put it to good use, and walking and walking, the bag getting lighter and lighter, and you walked faster then, your mind off on its own, and the plain brown wrappers, surprising how many there were, and Allie still getting them after the sex sugar debacle. Mack, who else, that found the ad at the back of the scanty jotter, Gentlemen, for the special lady in your life, guaranteed to make her want it as much as you do, and Nate, nobody living wants it as much as you do MacKenzie, and Mack ignoring him, we'll get it sent to you Allie, your old dear won't notice with all the records you get, and now a year and more later, still every month, the plain brown wrapper, a catalogue or a free promotion or some daud or other, and Allie calling Mack for everything, getting porn mail for the rest of his life probably, and only a matter of time before his old dear can't help herself and opens one, and Mack delighted with himself and not even trying to hide it.

And when the sex sugar actually arrived, all of you hysterical in Allie's kitchen, the lassies had to have heard you, sat there in the living room right next door, and Mack, put another spoon in Waldo, and Waldo, there's six in there already, and he put another couple into all the mugs anyway, and through to the living room with the tray, Viscounts too and no expense spared, the lassies sat there giggling, when did anyone ever ask them round for a cup of tea after school, and the hushed conferences in the hall, I think it's working, did you see Conway crossing her legs, and Shell never so quiet in her life before, but in the end the Viscounts all tanned and the tea hardly touched and no wonder, the stuff not just ultra sweet but with a bogging aftertaste too, and you never knew whether Mack and Waldo ever really believed it would work or not, they tried to act all disappointed, you need to write and get our money back for us Nate, we've been ripped off like your old dear with the bogus milk boy, but they couldn't keep it going, you were all laughing so much at the stupidity of it.

And why wouldn't you, the team itself a kind of joke, not like real teams that were hard bastards and battled other teams, Joe would be fine obviously, and Waldo probably, he was mental enough for anything, but definitely not the rest of you, it was the real teams doing the doyling and you were just the ones that got doyled. And a proud history really, the Neil's Wheels Doyling and the Minehead Doyling, the Swamp Doyling and the Luggie Doyling and still counting, in fairness Neil's Wheels just Mack on his own, climbing up the stairs at the Nolly, and he always swore blind he never said anything to the guy, but who would know with Mack, he probably deserved it, and all the rest were one hundred per cent genuine team affairs, and the Swamp and the Luggie the best. The Luggie the time Stevie Tait was going out with Nora and signed on for the duration, a good guy Stevie but getting you into a rammy with some bunch of guys in the Vale, and he said you should all hide behind the trees and come out when he called for you, the element of surprise, and you all solemnly swore you would, and Mack, almost as soon as you took your positions, let's get the fuck out of here, and Stevie half a minute later, right boys come on out, and nothing, and then sees the whole bunch of you over the fence and half way up the Waterside Road already, ya bastards, and chasing you with all of them behind him, of course they caught you, bunch of smokers and unfit bastards that you were, and it was only a kiddie-on doyling really that time, you were still ending yourselves at poor Stevie when they grabbed you. But the Swamp was serious, Joe throwing up on the guy's bike, and then buggering off, they knew better than to mess with Joe anyway, and the rest of you left to face the music at closing time, running for it into the Swamp and stuck up to your knees in fuck knows what, the bikey-wikey boys wading in and kicking the shit out of you, and Mack, when you made it out to the road, totally honkus plonkus and bleeding, trying to tell the guy, they gave us doylings, they gave us doylings, and the guy, what son, I can't understand you and only the next day does anybody twig it, doylings is a team word, the guy had fuck all clue what it meant, though Nate said maybe the blood and tears and snotters should have tipped him off slightly.

And that still wasn't counting all the near misses, Mack a liability at the best of times, the disco at the nurses' home, even after you'd had to beg the guy to let you in, it was blindingly obvious you were underage for a twenty-one shop never mind a private do, and Waldo showing the police discount card, does this make a difference, eh no son, and somehow you got over the door eventually, and Mack, out of the blue to the big bruiser beside him, and never seen the guy in his life before, that guy up dancing looks like a bit of a bent-shot, and the guy, he's no a bender, he's ma mate, ah go roon the wards wi him, and Mack trying to placate the guy, within a bawhair of another doyling, and Nate exasperated, why does he have to do it, I'm serious, he'll get us all killed one of these days.

And then in Frankie's Place, you could tell the regulars were growling the moment you walked in, but Mack oblivious, gaun yersel Cindy hen at the first singer, and then the compere guy, next up is wee Bella, if you don't like her singing, just look at her legs, and big Alex, pree-tend yoor happee when yoor blooo, and best of order for wee Davie, he's working his way up through the clubs, and Davie's catchphrase, och it was terrible, and Nate, if he was working his way up and only reached Frankie's Place, he must have started in the shiter, but Mack loving every minute of it, hooting and shouting encouragement to all the turns, and the punters growling, and how you made it out of there alive was another miracle. And still the other week when he was totally HP, down the main street at three in the morning telling the polis don't gimme no shit, and even after Nate sweet-talked them, yes we're taking him straight home officer, still shouting it after them, don't gimme noooo shit, noo-ooo shit, and a charmed life was all you could put it down to.

Walking over and turning off the telly, it wasn't as if you really needed the information, that first time up on the board a total fluke, and you kind of knew it even at the time, nothing but total wipeouts the rest of that session and the next, and nowhere close yet to getting back on a clean-breaking wave, the swells kind of irrelevant just at the moment, and if you were honest you were glad, you didn't actually want it to be easy, it shouldn't be easy, but however strange it might seem if you'd had to explain it to anyone else the hunger for news of the swells just another part of the same intense feeling down in your guts, the craving to dedicate yourself now to this chosen task, to be vitally connected to it in every possible way, bracing yourself to a determined aim, the fervent love of rigorous discipline released from somewhere inside you, and part of it the desire for knowledge just for its own sake, for the holy joy of it, learning won through hard labour, real and enduring. And when you thought about it you'd actually seen something like it in nearly all the team and just never recognized it before, in Mack and Joe and Waldo and in Allie the sparkie too, when they worked on the old squibs you were driving, endlessly altering, talking, dreaming of fitting twin cams and re-bored engines and fuck knows what all, you'd never understood a word of it, but you understood now, or thought maybe you did, at least part of the feeling that might lie behind it all. And true enough there were times when it must have been just a chore, especially for Joe, an apprentice mechanic, and helping service all his old man's motors as well as his job, but most of the time it was maybe for them like this was for you, you actually felt a bit guilty about how bored you'd always been, the patter as they worked the only saving grace, especially if Waldo was involved, playing something he howked out from under the bonnet like a trumpet, just call me Mr Air Filter Blower, or pointing at a scabby old tennis ball on the garage floor, get that up my bum right now, totally random bullshit, I stand here as hollow as a piggy bank that's empty, my legs are as bold as the Eiffel Tower support struts, quotes from Sven Hassel novels, his entrails flapping like a gory flag in the wind, and songs, If I had a Skoda, every day would be the first day of death, and Killing me softly with a Lada, and Joe, when he snapped the head off a bolt, I'm too strong to work on motors, and Mack and Waldo all night in the Vale, I'm too strong to walk in the Campsies, I would break them, I'm too strong to get on the Waverley, I would sink it, and back and forth, I'm too strong for this, I'm too strong for that, it still seemed funny for a surprisingly long time.

That was all that you'd seen then but now you could see the fuller picture, the time Mack went to roll down the window of Davie Drennan's old man's Hunter and it shattered, him and Joe getting some big oil-smeared book out, the two of them working it out somehow, it was all hieroglyphics to you, off to the scrappie, and the thing fitted and working before Davie's old man got in from the back shift, in fairness you'd even been impressed at the time, but now you remembered the concentration, the application, and joy was the word for it really, as they figured it out and got it done, fear of big Shug Drennan only a secondary motivation, though surely in the background somewhere, you'd be overstating the case to deny it.

Straight back to the Mitchell after that first day, and now with an even clearer idea of what you had to focus on and what you could disregard, get practice handling the board in the white water first before you think of paddling out, stick to the shallower water, get used to catching broken waves and closeouts, getting trim on the board, your weight not too far forward or you pearl but not too far back either. And so driving out to Dunallan every chance you got, every hour of daylight precious, and an added delight to watch the swell and see if you'd been right, watching it and watching it before you went in, but not for you yet, you were pleased to start again right at the beginning, an honourable undertaking and just how it should be, and even in the wee diddy white water you felt something like rapture, deeply read in your own thoughts, your mind prompt and watchful, your faculties quickened and vigorous, your whole being connected tightly to the active universe.

Every time out feeling more benefit from the heavy mail bag and the hours of walking, and you hardly even felt the cold now, you had to look at the colour of your hands to know if you needed to get out of the water and up to the brief for a heat, your blood seeming to flow with its own pleasure, an unrelenting agency driving you on, and lying flat on your board you raised your head up and let your back curve, and felt the wee closeout wave glide underneath you, and then slid joyously down the broken face of it, the faster you got the more smooth and stable the roll, stomach pressed down on the board, head still up, and feeling the rhythm in successive waves, your hands firmly on the rails, using subtle shifts of your weight to direct yourself in. And then finally you were ready to stand on the board again, catching a closeout, and the wave placable, indulgent, as if you'd earned the right now to stay up there five seconds, six, and almost all the way to the beach, and straight back out to do it again, learning and always learning, the sea imparting its renovating virtue by the end of every session, the next time already an eager prospect in your mind.

But no avoiding it, Mack onto you about your fly jaunts off in the brief, gone all night half the nights and all day at the weekends, and with prime summer ale time coming too, and the changes in your appearance, you looked too healthy, and don't be turning gayfruit on us now Andy, you with no comeback but a riddie, and thank fuck for Joe, leave the man alone cuntyballs, it's his own business what he does, and Mack letting it go just like that, you didn't mess with Joe when he was defending someone else, the earnest, ardent look that came into his eyes, like when the wee neds were onto big Timothy, big harmless soul, and Joe not even that friendly with him then, but jumping right in the middle of them, and grabbing the first one he could, and pinned him against the wall, the wee guy terrified, and all his mates, sorry big man, sorry big man, and if they'd had two seconds to think about it they'd have taken Joe easy, eight or nine of them and vicious wee thugs, but he never gave them two seconds, hardly a heartbeat, the pure raw courage of it, you either had it or you didn't.

And maybe it was the Twechar blood, Jacko and MacQuillan the first time you saw it, first week of First Year, the two of them best pals so they said, and every chance they got kicking fuck out of each other, and when the Art teacher left for two minutes, and for all they knew coming back any second, totally no holds barred, chucking chairs and tables and trays of paint at each other, they just didn't give a fuck, and all the rest of you cowering at the other end of the classroom, even the Hillhead boys that probably fancied themselves up to then. And not just the battling but mental in every way, in English doing the scene from Tom Sawyer in the graveyard, two jumpers tied together for the dead cat, and not even the slightest attempt to do the scene, the two of them just slagging each other off, and each insult funnier than the last, and Mrs Fordham laughing as much as anyone, the cat boys, don't forget the cat, and MacQuillan picking up the jumpers and dangling them by a sleeve, get that stinking thing out of here, and lobs it right across the room, and thud into the far wall, the whole class hysterical and Mrs Fordham practically doubled up herself.

But Jacko never out of trouble now, anything you heard, headed inexorably for the Bar-L, and maybe that's what Mrs Bannigan was thinking of, taking you and Nate and Allie aside, I'm really glad Joe's going round with you boys now, he was in with a bad crowd before, and it was true, most of his old team with records already and even a couple at Lowmoss, you took the piss out of him so much these days you forgot too easy how handy he really was, it took something like that to remind you, and then you were proud all over again that he'd chosen to be your mate, the same pride you felt when you hardly even knew him, and before you were even signed on to the team, talking to him for two minutes at Andrea Davidson's party, and Nate the next day, Joe Bannigan says you're no a bad big cunt, and mocking the big stupid grin that came over your face, but you didn't even care. And that same party, Old Joe screeching up in one of the minibuses, getting Joe hauled out from wherever he was, right you, I mean it this time, get your bags packed and get to fuck, you never saw a family argument quite like that before, right out there in public, everyone gawping at the windows or round the door, and Joe, whatever it was that he'd done, neither up nor down about it all, just can I sleep at yours the night Waldo till the old bastard calms down.

That was before the move to the ranch at Shiloh, Old Joe's business finally too big to run from a Council house, but it was Shiloh by the time you were fully signed on and granted visiting privileges, the bits of engines and rusting body parts and motors and minibuses the length and breadth of the place, the Council already threatening to take Old Joe to court, serving notices and fuck knows what because it was supposed to be a green belt, and inside no expense spared, the big stone fireplace and chimney with the real fire, the place always roasting warm inside, and smelling of King and Kong, and their chew toys and bones scattered around the floors, but it wasn't a bad smell, it seemed right somehow, and always a treat to go there, all the stuff that no-one else had, the Betamax video and the spacies you could play on the telly, last Christmas up till yon time watching videos of films taped off the telly, Birth of the Beatles, and Waldo demanding a rewind of the bit where Brian

Epstein pokes his head round the door to make things up with Lennon, the big dramatic moment, and Waldo, do you wanna see some puppy dogs John, and then Papillon, Steve MacQueen starved and beaten and miserable, snuffling as he gets marched along, and Waldo again, I can't go to Devil's Island blocked up like this mum.

Then in the morning, all of you dossed out in sleeping bags on the floor, coming to with a drouth and a head like a toyshop, and Old Joe and Mrs Bannigan frying up in the kitchen, no bother to feed the lot of you, Old Joe shouting through, anybody for fried beans, and Joe the only taker, aye, I'll have fried beans da, and Old Joe, naebdy for fried beans Eileen, and smiling, fair chuffed with himself when you all cracked up. Joe passed out from the bev in the afternoon, and no point in trying to wake him, the deepest sleeper there ever was, and lashing out, eyes still closed, if you tried to shake him, time for the team wade to the Vale, and Old Joe, please boys, can you no take Action Man with you. And it was always like that, Mack and Waldo helping them move from their old place, and Old Joe, just you let the boys do all the work Joe, it's only your stuff we're moving here, rolling his eyes at the two of them, I'm telling you boys, I've seen mair brains in a pun o shite, and when Joe pointed at his napper, see the knowledge that's in this dome da, Mrs Bannigan in on the act, aye maybe some day you'll let us all see what you know, Joe.

All of it another kind of code, the family close and loving too, and Old Joe and Mrs Bannigan always so kind to all of you, and second only to Allie's old dear in putting up with the team presence, even the most bogus stuff, improper use of their video, Mack straight up to the counter, what's the porniest movie you've got, and the guy, well I've got some through the back, but he must have been at it when he gave you The Love Gambler, and then Joe's big sister and wee sister coming in and Joe, unabashed, away through to the room, we're watching porn, Nate bestowing a softcore career on many a celebrity, fuck me, that's Daley Thomson, that's Bob Willis, and take your socks off Bob, ya clatty bastard, and then the Love Gambler at the track explaining the racing game to his blonde bit, this one's three to one odds but this one's ten to one odds and I like the jockey, and Nate with the lager coming out his nose, get yourself to fuck Love Gambler, the horses another thing Nate knew about, and putting the odd line on these days at the wee Mecca near the Uni, always cursing his luck, fucking Carson, couldny ride his wife, and the Love Gambler finally loving and losing it all, the last line of the film, oh shit, and Nate all the rest of the day, every opportunity, I like the jockey, and oh shit.

And what was most precious, a side to Joe himself that you felt privileged to see, the day your mum had all the folk from the union round and Joe thumping at your front door, bursting for a slash, the usual big loud voice, Andy, I need to use your hole in the ground for watering the daisies purposes, all embarrassed when he saw all the faces, I'm really sorry Mrs Duncan, and truly worried she would think badly of him, and your mum, ach you're totally fine Joe, I hope you know you're always welcome in this house, and her face warm to let him know how much she liked him, and that she thought highly of him, and you could see it meant something to him, and it meant something to you too.

4

The brief giving its familiar shudder, and the unhappy knocking from somewhere in its innards, and you didn't even have to look at the speedo to know that you just hit forty-five, you eased the guttie down on the accelerator, a practised veteran, the noise subsiding, the shaking ever less violent, waiting for it to hit sixty, and you didn't have to look at the speedo for that either, the poor wee squib could hardly go much faster. But that was fine, its own identity, hating forty-five, tolerating fifty, loving sixty, and Mack and Joe said it was common enough, its cruising speed, and maybe best not to mess with it, and you had no intention of messing with it, leave the tricked-up engines and the fancy driving to them, just gone four in the afternoon, plenty of daylight left, and sailing down the M8 already bound for Dunallan.

One of Allie's compilation tapes in the stereo, full volume, and you ran through the things in your head, bag safely up in your room, more than your job was worth to lose the bag, thermos of boiling water and plastic drum of cold water loaded in the boot, face cloth, shampoo, soap and towel in the poly bag, tiredness not quite lost yet from the two routes done in jig time, and practically running round, a big swell promised, the biggest yet, and you couldn't wait to see it, only a shame you couldn't get the afternoon bag before two, but no point in crossing management or the union, or your mum and dad come to that, that would be the worst of all, showing up the other workers, they'd kill you for that, son or no son. And anyway, you got everything you could out in the morning, the heavier the better, and the afternoon one always light, legs a blur, no problem to keep the bag overnight, they all did it, and your Manager, just keep it safe for fuck's sake Andy, and that was it, everything in place, and the wee brief cruising now, and Various Punks still blasting, and hitting its stride too, you had to hand it to Allie, John Cooper Clarke, the Kung Fu one, kicked in the balls while your assailant mutters something profound, you laughed out loud at those lines not for the first time, and the Buzzcocks, bdum bdum, that bit made you smile too, a catch-phrase of Allie's, and Wire, I am the fly, I am the fly, doing the accent and singing at the top of your lungs, and then The Jam, In the

City, a thousand things to be said, and all of them at a thousand miles an hour, the exhilarating rush of it, and The Jam really that got you interested in any of it, Fourth Year and sitting beside Nate in History, you didn't know then it would get you signed onto the team, just enjoying Nate's company, all the things he knew about, and loving that he had his own sarcastic take on most of them.

And that was the shocking thing, how open and excited he was about punk music, wide-eyed nearly, it took you by surprise, and you actually arguing with him when he quoted Weller at you, you'd heard fuck all yourself, the Ramones or something maybe, but still you waded in, maybe it was your mum talking, what if he should give two fucks about the guy's review, what if the guy was right, and Nate, exasperated, trying to explain it to you, it didn't matter if the guy was right or not, it was not giving the two fucks that was the whole point, and just doing the thing anyway, but you stuck to your guns and you were actually quite pleased with yourself, you maybe held your own with Nate for once. And then listening to the radio late on the Friday, Dr Dick interviewing Elvis Costello, the guy calling in to say he loved Way Down, you know the one, Elvis, you made it just before you died, and Dr Dick, sorry Elvis, a joker on the line I think, but Elvis was brilliant, the belief in himself and his songs burning through the wee diddy transistor you had in the bedroom, and then you saw him on Top of the Pops, The Angels Wanna Wear My Red Shoes, it was the best title ever, and the sound of the words so fantastic, hardly caring even what they meant, love getting fractured, and Elvis punctured, it was what you got for chasing after vengeance, he wore big glasses and sweated a lot, complexion green, jacket too big for him and tight drainpipes and toes pointed in and you thought he might actually be a wee bit deformed, but the utter commitment to the song and getting it across, it was giving everything and not giving two fucks right at the same time, and you thought then you knew maybe what Nate meant, and you started listening to Street Sounds on a Wednesday night and Nate said you were a dense bastard but better late than never.

Listening to Street Sounds hardly a stretch for you truth be told, you'd tuned in to Radio Clyde for years, first and foremost Tiger Tim, the Aff Its Heid Show on a Monday night, and amazingly the Tiger actually an apprentice in one of your dad's classes before he got his break on the radio, and said in an interview that if he hadn't been a deejay he'd have been an electrical engineer, and your dad, aye that'll be right, but he liked him too, you couldn't not like the Tiger, always falling off his chair according to your dad, he'd wear leopard-skin breeks to class, or a big ten-gallon hat with an arrow through it, and you remembered him at the kids' Christmas Party at the

College, making one of the lecturers go out first and get you all to shout we want Tiger Tim, we want Tiger Tim, and you didn't even know who you were shouting for, no-one had ever heard of Tiger Tim then. And now on the Tiger Tim Show, it's time for you to have a go, and show us all what you can do, when you sing along, in I'll Sing One For You, and wee lassies would phone in and sing along to the Theme from Mahogany or To Sir With Love, or just whatever was in the charts, and Tiger, have you got a boyfriend Linda, oh aye Tiger, is he a good kisser, the lassie in fits of the giggles, and you could hear her pals in hysterics too, och you're terrible Tiger, and once when a request came in from Barrassie, the bold Tiger, I bet it's a right brassie living there, you didn't know grown-ups knew about brassies, and you could write in every week and ask for a Tiger Tim Type Tune, and that was a choice from a couple of singles and the B-sides that someone had let him record himself, they were terrible needless to say, but the Tiger was brilliant, you couldn't not like the Tiger. And Dr Dick's Midnight Surgery, so bad it was good, competitions and records for prizes, and the dodgy double entendres, would you like a twelve incher Janice, consider it coming, the tactful late night conversations, are you married Jean, eh divorced actually Richard, oh I see, didn't work out then, and the same guy actually did the sports broadcasts too, a reputed Bluenose, and according to Nate one day actually forgot himself on air, Derek Johnstone right through, only the keeper to beat, and Johnstone must score, he's fucking missed it, but you never knew if that was true or just Nate, he wasn't exactly a fan of Dr Dick.

But Street Sounds something else again, you would actually try and get your mum or Louise to tape it for you if you had to be out for some reason, you didn't want to miss anything, not just the records but the people that wrote in, a whole feeling about it of something happening when nothing else was, Che Guevara that wrote in for months, and then one night, comrades, I have to announce that I can no longer bring the tidings of revolution to the airwaves as I have got a job at Coopers Fine Fare and they are making me work Wednesday nights, and The Tepids from Cumbernauld, they may or may not have been an actual band, putting humpty in front of everything, play Eddie and the Hot Rods again Ford and you'll get humpty laldy, that song's humpty mince, and Mr Very Evil, better and funnier than anyone, and a guy writing in trying to call himself Mr Incredibly Good, and a girl replying the very next week, she had shagged him and he wasn't. Brian Ford letting people say whatever they wanted, no censorship as far as you knew, and playing everything too, not just The Clash and The Jam and The Pistols, but Tom Petty and Dr Feelgood and Blondie, and The Skids and The Rezilloes and Spizz Oil, The

Lurkers and The Ruts and The Drones, Rubber Cars by The Wasps and Snatch, All I Want, and Devo and you name it, when the Evening Times did a feature on the show they called him The High Priest of Punk and half the letters the next week starting Dear High Priest, he read it out faithfully every time, he knew it was bollocks himself.

And then the disappointment of that too, wee guys going around with ripped clothes and safety pins, Stranglers tee shirts and shouting stick my fingers right up your nose, it wasn't as if you were any kind of original punk yourself, whatever that was, but something gone already, a lot of the bands still good and some great new ones too, but something still gone, why was it Peter Cook presenting Revolver on the telly, and him laughing at the music, slagging the bands, and your mum and dad agreeing, they liked Peter Cook, he was left wing, and the worst of it that they were right in a way, the bands sounding terrible, like they really were playing in a garage, and maybe fine if you were there but you weren't, and even Nate, and he liked Peter Cook too, having to agree with you that you'd all been shafted with that one.

Pushing the eject button on the stereo, onto the A1 now, only another twenty minutes or so before the first glimpse of the sea and Dunallan, and time for something different, Allie's tape flicked onto the passenger seat, and the new tape in, Graham Parker, and that's all that's left between you and me, yeah that's all that's left between you and me, something magical captured that couldn't be repeated, and he even said so himself on the liner notes, they could never get it again and the track on the album was the original demo, and then Steve Forbert, going down to see his girlfriend in some crappy wee town, and the sense of possibility he got into it somehow, first track on a great album, every song on it crackling with energy, and then the Modern Lovers Live, and the bit at the end where the beat speeds up, and the bass and guitar just play like percussion and the crowd clapping in time, and Jonathan, now's the time to have faith in what we can do, and no need to fear, and the beat speeding up more and more, and all the crowd clapping louder now, and then Jonathan, goodni-ight, the word taking on a resonance that was hard to explain, and you didn't know if it was the speeded-up beat or the audience clapping or the words that came before it, but it seemed to draw a line under something, like the message was given and now it was up to you, and always trying to hear it in the last few minutes before you got to Duke's and got your gear together to go out.

And it felt like you'd always been in thrall to lyrics in some way or other, getting the daffodils poem in English and even Nate thought it was boring, but you loved it, and you read it over and over, and you had it memorized without even trying, for oft when on my couch I lie, in vacant or in pensive mood, they flash upon that inward eye, that is the bliss of solitude, and it was like the antidote to stick my fingers right up your nose, the daffodils more alive in the guy's mind than when he saw them with his eyes, and then my heart with pleasure fills, and dances with the daffodils, the awesome power of a mind like that, and down the Kirkie Library, they had a big bastard of a Collected Works, and a smaller Selected Works, and you took the Selected Works.

And what a disappointment, hardly better than nursery rhymes half of it, idiot boys and shepherds and raggedy old dossers staggering around the countryside, you skimmed right through it and all set to take it back pronto, the daffodils must have been a fluke, and then right at the end, the bits from The Prelude, it was the daffodils with a hoover up their arse, and you went back for the Collected Works and read the whole Prelude eventually, looking up words, rapture and opprobrium and sublime, and bits of it sticking in your head too then, our destiny, our nature and our home is with infinitude, and only there, with hope it is, hope that can never die, effort and expectation and desire, and something evermore about to be. It set your own mind dancing, something evermore about to be, up with your dad on the road by Gartconner, your dad a city dweller all his days till then, and looking around purposefully, and you loved him for that, you knew he had no clue, and the guy with his own wee son, are you after cheggies boys, and your dad, yes you were, the guy telling you where the big tree was on the Gartshore Estate, and the sun that day, the sky pure blue, lying on your back on the grass, tired out with joy, your dad still heaving big useless sticks up at the cheggies, and you looked up at the pure blue of the sky through the leaves, gold and yellow and rust brown and red, and something evermore about to be.

Sure enough, a few years later, and it seemed a lifetime then, back in the exact same spot, and it could have been the same day, the sun and the leaves and the sky, you and Quinn out for cheggies, looking up and remembering, Gartshore discovered by you and your dad, you were proud of that, and becoming the family picnic spot for a while after that first time, cycling up on your bikes, your dad in front and your mum at the back, you and Louise in the middle, the wee tartan box fixed to the back of your bike so you could carry your fair share of the picnic stuff, and always touch and go if your dad could fix the puncture or whatever on his old bike in time to make the trip, the joy and relief when he would announce that he'd patched it up again somehow, playing football on the grass beside the tree, and beating your dad by the odd goal, you felt manly and grown up, Louise and your mum watching, and now you and Quinn, really and truly grown up so you thought, just started First Year, something wrong with the tree and the spiky cheggie husks were brown, just wee kernels inside them when you broke them open, but the tree itself and the leaves just the same, your heart full, looking up at the sky and remembering, your home with infinitude.

And you and Quinn then, two peas in a pod everyone said, switching to Woodilee for the cheggies, kicking happily through the leaves on the road, hour after hour heaving sticks up there, the thrill when an actual cheggie came down every once in a blue moon with the stick, and you didn't even know where the time went, always trying to build the perfect den down along the Luggie or the summer shooting at cans and targets in Quinn's back garden with his old man's air rifle, and Quinn still a good mate, he actually had some classes with Nate at the Uni, and quasi signed on with the team, but always with Elaine now, he was severely lumbered, and never so close anyway since the end of First Year, you never really knew exactly what happened.

That summer after the daffodils and The Prelude, and actually walking up to Gartshore and to Woodilee, and along the Luggie, and trying to feel it, and even saying it into yourself, our destiny is with hope, our home is with infinitude, but it wasn't there, why would it be, Wordsworth said it himself, he was a chosen son of Nature, singled out and special, and why bother with what a thousand hearts had already felt and every man alive could guess. And now carrying your board back up the beach, the waves sure enough the biggest and best you'd seen yet, but still you weren't quite ready, almost teasing yourself, staying in the broken waves and the closeouts and the white water, the fervent love of rigorous discipline, and everything in its proper place, knowing you were paddling out to the lineup next time no matter what, and your spirit totally peaceful, ready to face it when it came to you, standing at the car and peeling down your wetsuit, shivering, the hot water and a bit of cold for your hair, and then all of it into the cold, the edge taken off it, and a good rub down with the face cloth, the legs of the wetsuit peeled off now, everything brisk and businesslike the way your dad used to do it at the Kirkie Baths, and the fuckers always left the outside door bolted open in the changing rooms so you would freeze, standing in the hot shower for ages and never wanting to come out and face it, but no option here, and you liked that, it was part of it, shivering and drying yourself briskly with the towel, the car engine running already, and the heater on full, the pure clean feeling with your clothes back on, pouring the rest of the water over your wetsuit and drying it off diligently with the wet towel, looking forward already to the wee brief all warm and the drive back to Duke's garage.

And then best of all the drive back home, just tuck in behind a big truck and coast, watching his lights, every part of your body exhausted, the sheer deliciousness of it, the surge of every wee broken wave alive in your mind, every glide and turn of the board, and your own control of it, greater and greater every session, gliding and turning wherever the wave allowed you, small precise movements and practised weight shifts, and you and the water, the water's energy and your energy, fused together and working as one. English in Fifth Year a different thing again, Nate sat beside you there too now, you were just about ready for the team, and words a different pleasure from before, The Catcher in The Rye, Nate's favourite, and not a bad sentence in it, everything exactly right, and exactly how you felt, not lifting you up like Wordsworth did, but just telling exactly how it was, surrounded by bastards and phonies, you couldn't wait to leave it behind, and yet somehow missing everyone too the moment you thought of them, and Nate lent you Goshawk Squadron, bloody old Finlayson, hate the bastard, and have you kicked Helmsley's arse yet, take a good swing, wear boots, and Hemingway your set text in the class, everyone complaining except Nate, he got the point of it, and you got a bit of it too, real man talk, you kind of wished you could be like that, lines that stuck in your head, and it was fun to do them with Nate, it ruins the stomach and makes the hand shake, just the thing for a surgeon, and you on cue, you recommend it, and Nate, I use no other, drink it down baby and look forward to being sick. Waldo sat with Allie at the desk right in front of you, always in trouble for swinging back in his chair to talk to you and make you laugh, the time at Christmas humming Mary's Boy Child as loud as he could, and Craigie prowling around the class, who's doing that, who's doing that, Waldo stopping when she got close, but Mack already started on the other side of the room, and then Nate and you and Allie and just about all the boys in the class eventually, Mary's Boy Child stopping and starting all over the shop, and Craigie running around mental, I hoped you boys would be a bit more mature than this by now, and finally just giving every one of you punishment exercises, the lassies looking on smugly, they really were more mature, and no point trying to deny it.

5

The lounge of the Vale, and you'd always sat in the lounge, easier to get served when you were underage, and anyway it was nicer there if you had lassies in the company, not that you did really, Nora if she wasn't going out with anyone, and Fiona the odd time she came in with Waldo, but that wasn't often, she always wanted a quiet night in, and if Quinn came out then Elaine would be there by definition, but no appearance from them since the Quinn and Elaine tape debacle. And Quinn himself was fine about it and even told you he thought it was quite funny but Elaine on the warpath, she was never going to speak to Mack again, and a big surprise to see them here tonight, Elaine making a point of getting them as far from Mack as possible at the table, but seemingly prepared to be in his company at least, and maybe Quinn talked her into it, he liked a pint with the team, and Mack with the hide of a rhinoceros on him, rattling away to Elaine quite the thing, and her glaring back at him, the odd yes or no the best he was ever going to get from her, not that he gave a fuck about that either. And Nora for some reason all buddy-buddy with Elaine, you wondered if maybe she was a wee bit pissed off with Mack herself after the Drumshants caper, and finding out the whole team knew all about it, but it was hard to see, it wouldn't be like her, she was usually well up for all the team's doings, and especially when it was Mack, and the various mishaps and the stories half the reason she hung around with you in the first place.

Loving your first couple of pints, the best part of any session and no two ways about it, the taste developing about half way down the first jar, Mack onto you as usual for looking down into your pint as you drank it, just a habit, and the drink just an added bonus anyway, a rapt contentment already spread right through you from the afternoon at Dunallan, your spirit soothed, and the thoughts of it would come when they were ready, for now asking only what was timely, and loving the present hour for what it was, the light of high endeavours glimmering at a distance in your mind and to see it you only had to close your eyes. But the drink taking its other effect too, through to the bar for the men's bogs, you wished you didn't have to go, always a gauntlet to run, nodding at Joe over at the spacies, and he hardly looked up at you, face a mask of concentration, and you could hear the machine, ha ha humanoid, he must have just lost a man and best not to look back over, and then Gribble bang in front of you, how's it going big man, and you told him you were fine, how's yourself, and Gribble, the fucking bird's up the stick, not looking best pleased about it but you said congratulations anyway and Gribble, some cunt's getting a doing, and you couldn't help yourself, how come Gribble, are you not the father, and Gribble, oh I'm the father, I'm the father all right, but some cunt's getting a doing, and you had no idea what to say to that, just jigged about to show you were bursting and pointed to the door of the bogs.

And stood near the door Geggie Thomson, but hallelujah, he just nodded at you, deep in conversation with some wee guy, and you could hear the guy saying he'd just got engaged, and Geggie, aye she's no a bad ride, I've had better, and the last time you saw Geggie, down on the sideline at the Waterside park, a cup game and a pretty fair crowd, and bawling at the top of his lungs, where's Jimmy Lumley, where's the man that beefed his auntie, and just as you thought you were home and dry jackpot, it's Doc Halliday, all right son, GTF what does that mean, and you tried the straightforward approach, eh is it get tae fuck Doc, the Doc taking a step back, squinting appraisingly at you through the misted-up specs, the elastoplast round the base of one leg, ah smart bastard is it, all right then smartarse, NFC

NFC, his chin thrust up at your face, and you had to admit you didn't know, and the Doc, NFC Nae Fuckin Chance, NFB Nae Fuckin Brain, YFR You're Fuckin Rubbish, and waving his hand airily at you, he was done with you and you were free to go, and when you came out, the Doc with some other poor guy from the lounge, the guy practically pinned to the wall, aye that cunt Rommel, I kidded him on, oh fuck aye, bastard thought he could take me on at the dominoes, I says Desert Fox is it, the guy's girlfriend sat there in the lounge wondering how long it can possibly take for a slash, you gave her a sympathetic nod as you came back in.

Janie and Lynne working as hard as ever and both very sexy in their different ways, Janie sardonic and funny and Lynne shy and delicate, and Joe preferring Janie, she liked him too, twice his age but always flirting with him, and Joe yon time, haw Janie, get the ales over here or I'll have to put you across my knee, and Janie, aye it would take a man Joe, all of you hooting and Joe with the riddie, but pleased really, she liked him for sure, always taking the order from him even when it was your round, and just laughing and slapping his shoulder the time he tried to put the tip down her cleavage. But all the rest of you loved Lynne, and Waldo claiming he was up to ten wanks a day from the thought of her, and Fiona, och Derek, it was all she ever said about any of it, even the time he was reading the ads in a jotter and asked her right in front of everyone if she wanted a clitoral stimulator, and Fiona, och Derek, the rest of you trying to keep a straight face, and his lurid tales of their sex life, she was up like this and I was up like this, acting the whole thing out on Allie's old dear's good chair, and once when you chapped at his door, bare scuddy and pulling on his breeks, fuck's sake boys, I was right in the short strokes there. Even when you were still at school showing you his carpet burns from him and Fiona shagging on the floor of his bedroom, trying to keep the noise down, his old dears right underneath them downstairs, and still his old man managed to walk in on them, and later, look, it's no problem to me son but just don't do anything that would embarrass your mother, and now the whole team, every time anyone fucked up in any way, you've embarrassed your mother.

But even Waldo surpassing himself up north in the caravan, him and Mack and Allie and a whole big team, everyone just having a laugh and tanning the bev until suddenly Waldo, a propos of fuck all, I've got the bird's knickers on by the way, and the rest of them, away to fuck Waldo, and eventually when they still wouldn't believe him drops his breeks, and sure enough a wee pair of red scants and a nice wee white trim, the material all stretched out over his bollocks and his big hairy arse, and apparently he got Fiona to give them an extra day's wear before he took them off her. And maybe it was still on his mind the other week, all of you with half an eye on Lynne as she moved around the shop, the poor lassie just trying to do her job, getting the drinks in for everyone, the lounge totally heaving from the good weather, her petite wee bum and her pretty, delicate face, and after Nate orders his round in, four pints of Tennents and two Tartan please Lynne, Waldo, sotto voce, aye and a pair of your scanty panties darling, and maybe you encouraged him when you all laughed, all of you thinking something similar if you were honest, you were all mad in love with Lynne in one way or another, and when it comes his round adding on a scants and grapefruit please at the end of the order, and Lynne, what's that, a Guinness and grapefruit, smiling shyly, puzzled at your embarrassed faces, but still thinking it was something quirky and funny instead of just pervy, and even Waldo didn't have the neck to repeat it, and thank fuck Nate said, it was the worst attempted chat-up line in history, and if that wasn't embarrassing your mother then nothing was.

All of that when Waldo was still talking to you, but him in the huff too for now, and the sooner you put Mackenzie out to stud the easier all your lives would be according to Nate, it was always him that was behind the trouble, and time his membership was looked into, and Mack when you told him tonight, ach he doesn't mean it, he knows he loves me really, and speak of the devil, in walks Nate with the lassie Gillian in tow, and you fancied her the moment you saw her, who wouldn't, you saw more than one head in the lounge turn round for a good swatch at her as she waded over to your table, the no make-up and the old faded jeans and the army jacket just emphasising how little help she needed to look as good as she did. And of course the first time she goes off to the bogs, and Nora and Elaine away with her, Mack to Nate, are you nipping her big man, and Nate, his most withering look, aye in my fucking dreams, he had no false pride about that sort of thing, and by the way none of the rest of you had any chance either, it was a pure fluke she was here, the Troops Out demo in Dundee and their bus breaking down just up the road, him offering her to stay at his the night and a train into town in the morning, and he was surprised himself when she was for it, and Nate, she's smart as fuck, and not interested in wee daft boys like us. And that was all anyone needed to say to Mack, the challenge laid down, turning the charm up full the minute the lassies came back, the bev going down and the decibels up, and the lassie Gillian laughing as much as any of you at the show Mack was putting on, and Quinn ending himself, Elaine's coupon more and more furious.

And in all fairness, you couldn't really blame Elaine, and it was Allie's fault as much as Mack's for having the fancy stereo, and the rest of you for grabbing the mic when you were steamboats and didn't even know what you were saying half the time, not that Mack had that excuse, he always seemed to know what he was up to, the sleekit bastard. Allie's doctored Sydney Devine tape the start of it, I wandered today to the hills Maggie, and Conway's parents showing up to check on their wee daughter's party just as he put it on, pleasantly surprised for about two seconds and then the horror on their faces, arseholes, bastards, fucking cunts and pricks, the start of Plaistow Patricia spliced in by the bold boy, and booming out of their stereo that probably never played anything more edgy than Mantovani in its life before, and when you saw the Blockheads at the Apollo the crowd chanting that bit over and over and Dury, I'm not impressed, they're easy words to learn, and there was one band that gave full value, no arguments about that. And then a tape getting made just about every other week so it seemed, Nate's reading from Climax magazine, Joseph of Arimathea tampering with The Ezekiel, and praise him who comes in the name of perversion, and Waldo with his monologues from Oor Wullie and the Broons, would you look at the size of Fat Boab's dick and fuck me, Daphne Broon's pregnant, and all of you with some gibbers or other, until finally this one that caused all the trouble, Allie with the mic set up and the usual drunken nonsense spouted into it, and it was inevitable the bold Mack would grab the thing sooner or later, and now we're pleased to present a recent recording by Phil Quinn and Elaine Bryden, and off he goes, oh Phil, oh Elaine, oh Phil, oh my clittie clittie, and poke my arse, poke my arse, and on and on, you were partly to blame for laughing so much, only a matter of time before that goes on at a party too, and you had to feel a bit sorry for Elaine, sitting through that, all her pals round about her, and a bunch of people she didn't even know hearing it too.

And so that was how it stood now, Elaine still drawing daggers at Mack, and Mack giving even less of a fuck than before, all his attention on Gillian, and Gillian hooting at him, her hand up to her mouth, and she looked even better when she laughed, her whole face vivacious and bright. Elaine of course with the face like fizz but now that you looked, Nora was none too happy either in fact, and there was one reason you could think of, she'd brought her share of lassies down to the Vale herself in her time, Linda and Helen and that Cynthia one, just looking for a bit of female support, and sure as fate Mack nipped them, or Joe maybe, and then pissed them off in one way or another and poor Nora back to square one, on her tod again with the lot of you, and now here it was happening even with this one of Nate's, and if that was it right enough, then she maybe had a point at that.

But anyway that was how it was, and Mack a force of nature as much as the tide, there was nothing for you to do about it any more than Elaine or Nora, you wished him well, and the lassie Gillian too, you hoped he would be kind to her, and you knew he could be when he wanted, and you sat back and let your mind go where it wanted now, this afternoon your first time on an unbroken wave since your very first day, and the angled take-off, you'd practised it session after session over the weeks in the broken waves and the closeouts, and today back out to the lineup, the sets a full foot higher now than on that miraculous day, your board at an angle to the shore, choosing your wave, the commitment made and no room for second thoughts, and then the practised movements, feeling your own grace and skill, everything fluid, all the parts moving in harmony, the wave picking up your board, and already sliding down the face as you got to your feet, crouching slightly, arms apart for balance, the angle racing you frontside now along the face, the wave peeling behind you, the water rushing under your board and the feeling like you were going faster than anyone had ever gone, and yet still in trim, all your hard work rewarded, the tiny shifts of weight to keep your speed and your line like second nature already, and you were a dedicated spirit, the wish for something loftier elevating you in that moment far above any pain or fear, and you felt it now as vividly as then, and you knew it wasn't the drink, or wasn't only the drink, and then you were back in the Vale, and glad to be back, your mates around you, and half the night still ahead.

Gillian asking Mack about this Waldo that you all kept talking about and Mack, now there's a subject, and what a touchy bastard Waldo was, and don't get me wrong, I love the guy like a brother, but come on to fuck, and telling her about Waldo's Valentine, the whole history, wee Geeshy Hamilton wrestling in First Year with Jimmy Bryant, and claiming that Jimmy touched up his balls, and whether Jimmy did or he didn't, that was the reputation he had all through school, and Mack and Joe on Valentine's Day just passed, getting a big huge card for Waldo, and then their inscription, your massive masculine boab has often been the subject of my masturbation fantasies, signing it JB, and round at Waldo's house, his old dear reading the one from Fiona and then it was show me your other one Derek, come on, don't be shy, and Waldo, no ma, and Mack and Joe, och go on Derek, show your mother your card, and don't be so sensitive, Waldo's dial lit up like a belisha beacon from embarrassment and fury at them.

Mack laughing so much himself at the recollection of it that he didn't even notice when Gillian stopped about half way in, and now frowning at him, the first time she'd said much more than please and thank you, and Gillian, I think guys that are always going on about poofs and benders are maybe not that sure of their own sexuality, and Elaine nodding her head off, hear hear, and even Nora smiling a wee bit, and Mack, fuck I never thought of that, turning round to you with a big leer on his dial, what about it then Andy, you fling it up my arse in the bogs, and I promise to tell you if I like it, smiling his smile at Gillian, he thought he could just charm his way out of anything, and not even noticing that she still wasn't having any of it but straight on to Waldo's latest, and why he was in the huff up in the house, miserable with Fiona instead of out with his mates where he belonged.

Just a perfectly innocent conversation, a few of them over at wee Brim's house, and for some reason onto the subject of names, and Waldo, Wallace is a pure Scottish name by the way, my old man's traced our family right back to the original clan, and no-one disputing it, why would you, it was obvious enough, William Wallace and whatever, but on and on, Wallace this and my old man that and pure Scottish the other until finally Mack, ach away to fuck Waldo, your old man's a darkie, and instantly Waldo taking the huff, say anything you like about me, but don't you start on my family, that's totally out of order Mack, slamming the door in high dudgeon, and even when Allie tried to bring his share of the home brew round, Waldo swilling his finger around in the bucket, they've pished in that Allie, and insisting on tipping the whole lot of it down the pan, and as if anybody would pish in the man's lager, but Waldo on and on, and if you saw his old man, the guy was the colour of a big raw chip, you couldn't remotely mistake him for a darkie, but still on and on, they pished in my lager, they called my old man a darkie, and all you could do was wait for the daft bastard to calm down. Mack shaking his head and laughing, and the slightly puzzled look just starting to come into his eyes as he finally notices the expression on Gillian's face.

And then Gillian standing up, her bonnie mouth tight with rage, I'm not going to sit here and listen to any more of this racist fucking poison and off to the bogs, Elaine and Nora right behind her, and an awkward silence, Mack giving it the what did I say routine and Nate as cool as ever, ach I told her you were a bunch of useless bastards, and Joe, fuck this, I'm away to play the spacies, Allie as usual keeping his thoughts about it all to himself, and you didn't know what inspired you, probably thinking of what your mum would say if she knew you were putting up with words like darkie, and more than putting up with them, a fully active participant if you were honest, it wasn't exactly the first time you'd heard the story, and laughing your head off every time, she would be saying a lot more than Gillian that was for sure, she'd be ashamed of you, and you actually felt ashamed of yourself, and before you knew it you were saying we were well out of order there Mack, we should apologize when the lassies come back, and then you felt everyone's eyes on you, your face hot with the riddie, and then Mack, the big cheesy grin spread across his coupon, ah it's like that is it, well you've got good taste big man, I'll give you that, and before you could even deny it the lassies coming back, and Mack, his eyes all lowered and contrite as a choirboy, eh Gillian, I just want to say that I owe you an apology for my eh racism and eh anti-gayness and that, and then telling her how it was Andy here that had straightened him right out and no mistake, and that he was really and truly and sincerely sorry, and then turning to you, all deferential, is that okay Andy, and what else could you do, you said it was fine as far as you were concerned and that you were sorry too, and Allie, I'm sorry too, and Nate, shaking his head at the lot of you, shower of useless bastards, what did I tell you Gillian.

But Gillian just smiling, the obvious sweetness of her nature, and she said she wanted to apologize herself for losing the rag, I mean it's me crashing your company, and how Norman was doing her such a big favour letting her stay at his house, and it was all you could do not to smile yourself at that, only Nate's old dear and the teachers at the school called him Norman, but Gillian looking at you pretty damn gratefully too, and surely she didn't really believe that pile of bullshit from Mack, but anyway there it was, Elaine looking a bit disappointed but scootching in cat-like against Quinn, any kind of crisis was a good excuse, and him with a manly arm around her, Nora off to see if Joe needed a hand at the spacies.

The night over too soon, and a prodigious amount of bev tanned all round, and you noticed that Gillian could hold it, and you hardly felt it yourself for once, all the goodbyes said, and Gillian standing with Nate outside, the rest of you set for some party Joe knew about, taking a million years as usual to round yourselves up, and Mack grabbing you by the arm, and hauling you outside, hand on Nate's back and telling him he was needed inside, and you saw Gillian's eyebrows raised, it was such an obvious set-up, and Mack, if you're needing a good ice-breaker Gillian, get the man to tell you about his fly wee jaunts. And just like that, Mack away back inside and dragging Nate with him, and you and Gillian stood there together in embarrassed silence, and finally Gillian, okay, what about these fly wee jaunts then Andy, and the bev must have been affecting you more than you thought actually because for some reason that's all it took, and you started telling her about Dunallan, and about surfing, and Gillian, I didn't even know there were any surfers in Scotland, and you, there's a few of us, not many, and Gillian, so Mack knows about it then at least, and you, no, you're the only person I've ever told, thinking how strange it sounded even as you said it, but Gillian looking earnestly at you, and she said she felt privileged then, and that she'd really like to come and watch you some time if that would be okay, and that was when you knew you'd really lost it, because you heard yourself saying yes, and that would be great, and then there was nothing left but to go for it, the decision made instantly, like the decision to catch a wave, but still your voice faltering, actually Gillian, I was wondering, I mean, well eh, would you maybe like to maybe eh go out with me some time before then, I mean like to the pictures or that, waiting for her to say no, and of course she would say no, but actually she said yes, and I'd really like that, and even smiling warmly at you, and that was it, you were going out with Gillian Harper.

6

The euphoria of it lasting the whole next day and into the night, and then the anxiety, thinking about all the experience Gillian must have, and what she might be expecting from you, and fuck all the help to be had from Nate, when you phoned him to ask what he meant about her having no time for daft wee boys like yourselves he said he'd just been assuming, she was obviously nowhere near as smart as he'd thought, and if that was right you didn't even know if it was good or bad, and Mack the obvious person to ask about it all but you'd never ask him in a million years, or Waldo either for that matter. Casting around in your own experience for something you could use and the only thing that came to you was Primary Six, and fuck all the help that was either, a wee group of the Primary Seven lassies huddled up in a circle, belting it out at the top of their lungs, cum on feel the noize, girls shag the boys, giggling hysterically and hooting, and what you were feeling now barely different from what you felt then, excitement and curiosity and bewilderment and fear, and the excitement blowing all the rest into the weeds, that was something at least.

Karen Clarke at the Second Year prize-giving, that definitely was something, in her class the whole year and never talked to her once, but none of you talked to lassies then, the fear of being called a poof, whatever that was, some kind of big jessie, and Mack the only exception, never done giving them his patter even at primary school, and never gave a fuck what anyone thought, the bastard was sniffing even then according to Nate. But you always liked Karen, the look of her, and the confidence of her, her school tie tied in a big huge knot with a wee silly tail sticking out underneath, it looked ridiculous, and a week later everyone in the whole school was tying it like that including you, and you never knew if she actually started it or if she just helped make it popular, she stopped wearing a tie pretty soon after that anyway. Still all you could think was how unlucky you'd been to get put between two lassies, Karen on one side of you and some other lassie on the other, it must have been alphabetical, and actually relieved when they got the thing started, the minister from up the road was the compere, and there's an old gypsy legend, he says, that if a newborn child is kissed on the eyes, then that child will have the gift of vision and be a great artist, and if a child is kissed on the lips then that child will have the gift of song and be a great musician, and you thought aye right, maybe just sitting in silence with a big riddie wasn't so bad after all, but then he said he didn't know where he was kissed himself but the Rector had told him he was just the man to chair these proceedings tonight, and you thought that was pretty funny actually, you noticed that Karen laughed too, and in fact things brightened up whenever the minister came on to do his wee turns in between all the other stuff. But what a carry-on the rest of it was, first the Rector, then wee Morrison, then Taylor, then some arse from the PTA, a good hour gone by and fuck all the prize given to any bastard, and then it was give a big welcome please for the school choir with Some Enchanted Evening, and Karen's voice right next to you, the first words out of her mouth all night, aye some enchanted evening right enough.

Laughing out loud then, you couldn't help it, and Karen smiled at you and blew at the wee wisp of hair on her forehead and rolled her eyes, the two of you talking and never stopped the rest of the night, the wee crabbit guidance teacher with her head leaned over from the end of the row hissing at you to be quiet, and the chance of that was buds, you never talked to a lassie like that in your life before and no idea how it even happened. Too bad in a way for the summer holidays, you hardly even saw Karen around the place once Third Year started, and ready to put the whole thing down as a fluke until the practices for the Christmas dance, all the guys lined up on one side of the gym and all the lassies on the other, and there she was, she caught your eye and blew the wee wisp of hair up again like she'd done before, you tried to be cool the first time and just saunter over there and of course some guy got in before you, and the next time you just ran over mental and made sure you got her, you weren't giving a fuck, talking and laughing just like before, making a total arse of the Gay Gordons and the St Bernards Waltz, the teachers shouting one two three up down and fuck knew what, you were trying to talk above them, and when they said it was a ladies' choice Karen came and got you, you were beaming with the pride of it, and even though there was no need for her to come horsing over like you did, there wasn't exactly a competition for you, she moved pretty smartly anyway, you loved her for that, and actually you were one of the first guys picked.

But the disappointment when you said something about dancing together at the actual dance and she said she wasn't going, she had a boyfriend in Fourth Year, and of course you should have known that a lassie like her would have a boyfriend in Fourth Year, he wasn't allowed at your dance and she said he didn't want her going without him, and the first thing you ever saw about Karen that you remotely didn't like was that she looked quite pleased about the fucker telling her she couldn't go, you still danced the rest of the practices together and still had a laugh but it wasn't the same, an effort actually to be light and friendly when you would see her in the corridor or the playground after that, and Mack not that long ago in the Vale telling you she was engaged, and for all you knew it was to the same fucker that didn't want her dancing with you, and Mack, did you not have a thing for her Andy, you tried to deny it through the big riddie, the bastard must have had flash cards or something for that stuff, he never forgot anything. And actually you remembered Mack too at that Third Year dance, no idea then that you'd ever be in his team, or Waldo's either, the two of them seemed so far ahead of you, Waldo away off with Christine Barr and winching her in a corner of the big games hall, and with the teachers there and everything, and Mack the only guy in a crowd of lassies, easy as you like, you walked past as slowly as you could, he was asking them how you said fellattio, that was how he pronounced it, all the lassies hooting, and one of them, all pleased with herself, it's fellayshio, Robert, you could only admire it, he could probably have had a blowjob right there just by asking them how you did it.

And all through Third and Fourth Years and into Fifth Year the two of them like a double act, Waldo with just one bird at a time but he always had one,

Christine for a few months then Carolyn and Valerie and finally Fiona, and it seemed like there was never even a day in between any of them, and meantime Mack seemingly working his way through the whole Year, and when he got a rubber ear he would boast about that too, and just as friendly with the lassie as ever, he said you had to give them the chance to correct their mistakes. Then the parties starting to happen, and for some reason it was just lassies that had them, Mack always invited of course, Allie too, and Waldo and Nate to most of them, drinking cider and playing Postman's Knock, you had the girls shag the boys feeling whenever you heard the stories from Nate, and at one of them they played strip poker, it wasn't poker really, just a card dealt to everyone face up and the lowest card had to take something off, everyone ending up in their underwear, and then Shell got the lowest card two deals running, off with the bra, and no-one thought she would do that, and then incredibly the scanties too, straight back on with both of them fair enough but still sat there totally bare scud for those few seconds, the lassie that sat right in front of you in Physics, and Nate said they all just sat about shivering for a while after that, and Mack with the obvious big brickie plain as day through his Ys, not the slightest effort to cover it up, taking in all the details for a good wank later, and the poor lassies didn't know where to look, though truth be told more than one of them sneaked a peek at the thing.

All of it a constant reminder of how far behind you were yourself, but still glad you were around courtesy of Nate when Waldo announced he'd had a wank under the table to Ruby Redford in French, the finger and thumb method was the business for it he said, and wee Geeshy sat next to him didn't even notice he was doing it, Ruby in the wee short skirt as usual stretching up to write irregular verbs and whatever on the board, and definitely the most humpable of all the teachers, but still only Waldo would decide it was a good moment to have a pull, and he said she might even have had some idea what he was up to, he was pretty sure he seen her nipples hardening now that he thought about it. Nate snorting and shaking his head, and he said maybe Waldo could do wee Barrett in Home Economics next, she was about forty and twenty stone, and Waldo, deadly serious as far as you could tell, wee Barrett, oh fuck aye, she's a wee ride, all of you cracking up at that one, you were grateful to be included in it, and then Nate finally wangling you an invitation to Diane MacParland's party, you were determined to dive in and make up for lost time, round to the offie with the big man and he told you to wait outside, you were too young-looking, and in he goes, the big list with everybody's orders on it, and the poor lassie chasing around all over the place behind the counter, it's all one of this and two of that, lager and heavy and export and pale ale, Carly Legopener and Nookie Broon and fuck knows what all, and when she's finally got it all on the counter, he hands over everybody's old crumpled notes and coins and starts loading it up carefully into the big muckle rucksack, nothing suspicious about it at all, the lassie even giving him a hand, and nobody but the big man could have done it, it was just the air he carried about with him.

Then the sheer good luck of it, you'd hardly even noticed the lassie before but obviously she was there in the exact same spirit as yourself, all set for getting off with somebody no matter what, and thank fuck you were well loosened up on the couple of tins, Waldo telling you in the kitchen to get the Carly Crowbar down her throat as well, you were proud to get advice from him, and when the lights went out down onto the floor, other couples both sides of you and at your head and feet, for some reason it didn't seem that strange, winching and groping each other over your clothes, you could tell she was a beginner at it like you were, your teeth were banging together at regular intervals, but when you moved your hands down tentatively to feel her bum through her jeans you felt her breathing get harder and heavier and you knew that was a good sign, and not much later you came yourself, you wondered if she had any idea, and probably not, she kept winching you as ferociously as ever, and you tried to carry on like nothing had happened though you could feel that you were breathing harder yourself now.

And that was the start of your wee run with Lyndsey, you must have said about ten words to each other over the four or five parties, struggling to come up with anything even when you were walking her home afterwards, but still always finding each other just before the lights went out, going a wee bit further every time, and you could hardly believe the excitement of it when you finally pushed her bra up under her top and your fingertips were touching both of her nipples, and you came instantly, you'd been winching her passionately for about two hours non-stop in the hope of it, and then it filtered through to you what was playing on the stereo, fucking Chris de Burgh, and Patricia the fucking Stripper, you actually felt quite depressed, you knew right away it was what you would always remember, and whether you gave some sign of it or whether she could just tell by now that you'd shot your load and your heart wouldn't be in it for a while, she reached her own hands up and pulled her bra back down, and adjusted herself and sat up, and the two of you sat there in silence listening to fucking Patricia and her hilarious fucking capers.

And lucky again really that Allie and Nate were on wee runs of their own at that same time, Allie discreet as always and just disappearing off into a bedroom with the bold Shell, but Nate would come over totally steamboats to give you the progress reports on some lassie or other, she's letting me go surprisingly far by the way, his big lanky frame swaying about dangerously, and he didn't care about Lyndsey hearing him, she thought it was funny anyway, and the few bits of conversation you ever had with her were usually after a bulletin from the big man, the time he broke off from winching his lumber to throw up into the glass, it wasn't even a pint, just a wee silly tumbler like your mum and dad had, you could see what was going to happen right away, and sure enough the stuff cascading over the rim and pouring down the sides, and it was actually that lassie's party, her parents all concerned and asking him if he wanted some bread and butter to settle his stomach, you nearly tossed your cookies yourself at that one, and walking up the road with him after, he was crashing at yours, the ice on the ground and the two of you slipping to fuck from that and the bev, and Nate, I might as well just join the army after this Andy, and how his old man was going to string him up with piano wire, the two of you crying with laughter it was so funny, and in the morning neither of you could even remember what it had been about, it couldn't have been the lassie, she was quite nice really and better than Nate's usual if truth be told. Not exactly a shock when you heard Lyndsey was going out with some guy, you hadn't seen her for a few parties and no intention of ever asking her out yourself, she would have been as miserable and uncomfortable as you, putting on the punk music in place of winching now, and you and Nate and Allie crashing around in the dark, shouting along with the lyrics, The Rezilloes loving their baby cause she did good sculptures or Richard Hell wanting out of here before he was even born, trying to avoid the bodies coupling on the floor, and not caring too much actually if you didn't, Waldo and Mack up for it too sometimes, and Joe later when he started hanging around with the two of them, and that was the start of you joining the team probably, most of every party just sat around taking the piss with Nate, you still knew you were missing out again but the edge definitely taken off it by the take he had on it all, big Porter coming out of a bedroom at Shell's party, swinging his used johnny around, grimacing and rubbing at his crotch, oi've been oggin ole noight and me boles are ikein, the pang of envy, it felt like pain, and instantly Nate, fucker probably wanked into it when she wasn't looking, it made you feel better somehow.

And whatever chance you had of not fucking up completely with Gillian more than likely didn't come from any of it anyway, Mack and Waldo to thank if you were honest, however loath you would be to ask them anything now, Waldo admitting you to the brotherhood of the briefcase before you were even fully signed on with the team, handing over the old knackered school satchel to you with all due solemnity, you knew it had been round the rest of them a good few times already, and you couldn't wait to get it home yourself, the thing stuffed to bursting with scanty jotters and some of it pretty hardcore, Waldo's whole collection plus the odd contribution from others, you had it a good couple of weeks hidden in your cupboard and through every page several times over, and actually you preferred the softer stuff or your imagination for the wanking, but the anatomy never so clear to you before, it put you straight at last on a good few points, and the stories not unhelpful either come to that, it seemed to you that you picked up a few things there too. And then Mack out of the blue telling you he needed you for a double date, and no idea why he thought you were the right man, you didn't question it but just went along, the lassie he was sniffing after wouldn't go out without her pal, and you winched the pal all through the picture while Mack was lumbering his lassie, she seemed content enough with your technique, and you weren't even surprised when she put her tongue in your mouth, the briefcase to thank for that, and you could hardly believe it had never occurred to you or Lyndsey in all those hours you were going at it, what the fuck were you even doing, you took more confidence from that one date than all your previous efforts, and not a lot to boast about at that, an old school bag full of porn and a lassie doing a favour for her pal, of course you never saw her again, and neither of you even had to say anything, you just thanked fuck that Gillian didn't know anything about any of it, and the truth was you felt hardly a minute further on from girls shag the boys, and all you could do was worry and hope.

7

Respite from the vain perplexity of it never more welcome, and you were never more grateful for Dunallan, driving out for session after session, and the bottom turn to learn, taking off at an angle all well and good if all you ever wanted to be was a passive receiver of the wave's tumultuous energy, taking and taking and only half-giving, a big part of your own energy still locked inside you, harnessing the spirit of the wave while your own spirit was held in check, your soul too timid to seek community with highest truth and highest expectation, and you knew you could never reconcile yourself to such a prospect, the zeal to somehow connect yourself to the full power of the wave awakened, summoned, roused inside you, the thirst for vigour all but unquenchable now, and you were daring to speak a higher language, fully wakeful to the love and beauty and fellowship rushing beneath you, the swell and the waves and the tide spreading through you a commotion like their own.

Sitting on your board at the line up, they were breaking just a few feet high, and that was about as much as you wanted right now, the spot chosen for its right-breaks, learn the frontside first, and then the backside, easier to face the wave for now, but there were left-breaks around too and you knew where they were, that was for later, a good thick coat of wax on the deck, and here was your wave, up quickly, you'd done it a hundred times before in the closeouts and on the angle, the action already becoming an instinct weeks ago, feet planted instantly and securely, and straight down the face for the very first time, a fresh exhilaration, and the water below your board honouring the bond invisibly given, the stages in the book from the Mitchell themselves just an acknowledgement of the secret vows taken by all surfers, the order of your progress through them ordained centuries ago, and the bond ancient and universal, the wave stern and honourable, releasing its energy to you now, keeping its promise as you knew it would, and at the bottom you eased your weight onto your back foot and let the tail and the inside rail of your board find their own right space in the rushing water, and the fin slicing through, and you cleaved round and into trim along the face, faster than ever before, the wave extending to you its full speed and power, your heart exultant and impassioned, and yet a sense too of something far more deeply interfused, a confidence in the truth of it, and in the joy of it, and in the love of it.

And against the sureness of that bond and that love, the uncertainty and the worry and the fear, but still more than anything the excitement, the date finally arranged and Gillian saying she'd just meet you at the pictures in the town, you could maybe run her home, and she picked the film, Scum, it wouldn't have been your first choice yourself, but pretty good actually in the few scattered minutes when you could concentrate, the guy slapping black boot polish on his bare feet in the Borstal, pretending to be a vegetarian and refusing to wear leather shoes, and determined that they weren't having him, but in the end they got everyone, Gillian smiling affectionately at you when you took her hand and then kept holding it, and that seemed to be fine, but all the time worrying about what you should do when you got back to her flat, surely nothing to stop you when you were there, and of course you wanted to, but what if she didn't, or if she suddenly woke up and saw that you were just a daft wee boy after all, excited and bewildered and stood transfixed in the playground, and actually relieved when she said in the brief, I can't invite you in Andy, you wouldn't believe the squalor, and you relaxed for the first time all night, and then you had a good winch parked in the street outside, and Gillian in no hurry to go in either, and now you could go on the Tiger Tim show with complete confidence, she was undeniably a good kisser, but still you were relieved all over again when she said don't bother seeing me in Andy, you'd have had trouble moving with the brickie you had.

And your second date Elaine Bryden's eighteenth at the Hawthorne, and the second time you'd worn your suit in your whole life, the visit to Slater's to buy it for your job interview at the Post Office, the guy asking you about sleeve length, and when you took a wild guess he said yes, you were like him, you liked to show a bit of cuff, and then asking you what side you dressed to, and you had even less idea about that and just took another guess, the guy making a note in his wee book, and when your dad told you later what it meant and you looked at the suit, you couldn't detect the slightest difference on either side of the fly, it was an off the peg suit anyway, the alterations just to make it fit better, and you were in the dark to this day why he asked you that one, but the suit smart enough, plain dark blue, and you wore that and a white shirt and a knitted light blue tie, you couldn't even tie a Windsor knot in it, it came out too thick, and you had to tie a wee silly primary school one, you had no idea about clothes, and you thought about Nate's gallus wee brother, off to his Fifth Year school dance in a Boys Brigade cap, the ridiculous triangle one, his old man's polis shirt several sizes too big, and a kilt and Doc Martens, not giving a fuck.

But your whole mission in life as far as clothes were concerned always to just blend in and not be noticed, and loving that all of you in the team wore jeans and a Wrangler jacket, no-one actually called it a uniform, but you liked it for the same reason you liked the school uniform, though pretending to hate uniforms, everybody hated uniforms, and then Gillian, when you picked her up, in the lemon yellow dress, the skirt just below her knees, wee thin yellow shoulder straps, and her back and shoulders bare, and the white high heeled shoes, she looked miraculous, her skin freckled and tanned and her legs bare as well, and meeting up with the team in the Vale before the do, each and every one of you looking so good, you'd never have thought you could all scrub up so well, and when Joe saw Gillian, a hand on your shoulder, a sigh, and the sad rueful tone, what the fuck is she doing with you big man, and you didn't know yourself but you knew it was the best compliment Joe could give and you felt yourself puffing up with the pride of it, and even the taxi driver on the way to the Hawthorne looking at you enviously it seemed to you.

And a truly minted night, the deejay claiming for ages he didn't have any punk records, and you got up a few times with Gillian to the mince he was playing but even with the bevs in you it was no good, hopping from foot to foot and no connection at all to the so-called dance music, and Nate danced with

Gillian much more than you did, the big man could actually dance, fluid and natural, and even you could tell he was pretty cool, and Gillian like all lassies as far as you knew, elegant and effortless too, just moving her shoulders and her feet smoothly in time, and wiggling her bum a wee bit, and you could see of course that it was fun if you could do it like that, but then eventually, hallelujah, the guy putting on Plastique Bertrand, it wasn't great, or good even, but it was something, and all of you instantly up, jumping around mental, crashing into each other and hooting, and people gathering round the floor to watch and laugh, and more than a few coming on to join in, and the guy emboldened to try the Boomtown Rats, more people getting up, and even the wee table of Elaine's old dears and their pals up for it, and sure enough, it turns out that the guy's got The Jam and Siouxse and even finds Pretty Vacant and Blitzkrieg Bop from somewhere, and another great joy of punk music that the worse dancer you are the better, and Gillian shrugging at Nate, taking her shoes off and bouncing about as best she can in her good dress, and the two of you taking a break for one song, falling down together on the chair, both of you all sweaty, her arms around your neck and even managing a quick winch before the rest of them came over, Mack with a big tray of drinks, and Nate, drink it down baby, and look forward to being sick.

No taxis to be had of course, and only right that Elaine's old dears and their pals should get them anyway, walking back up the road past the Nolly, Mack without a lumber for once, and suddenly declaring it was time for the Canal Olympics, the stroke to be freestyle and first man across takes the honours, and Nate, away to fuck cuntyballs, there's dead weans and everything in there, but Mack already plunged in, his good suit, shoes, jacket and everything, and the filthy stagnant water not much past his waist, already scrunching down to make it look like he was swimming, wading across through all the hoach and stoor of it, the green slime on the top all churned up from the kiddie-on crawl he was doing with his arms, and as he gets to the other side reaches down and howks something off the bottom, the barrel of an old rusty exhaust and right, he says, this is the Canal Olympics Trophy, and I expect every man who is a man to get in here and compete for the honour of his bird. Wading back across and standing there looking up at the wee group of you, Waldo and Fiona, Nora and her new man, Joe and his lumber, yourself and Gillian, and Nate, all of you looking down on him disbelieving from the bank, and Mack, I'll just stay in here myself now I'm in, I'll let you useless bastards have a start off the blocks, and Nate and Joe all set to just turn and go, and Nate, aye that will be right, and you looked at Gillian, set for the road yourself and hoping she wasn't too pissed off and disgusted at Mack, and Gillian, don't even think about leaving this spot Andy Duncan, get your arse in that water and fight for my honour, and you couldn't believe it, you said really, and she said really, did you not see that beautiful trophy, and you saw her eyes alive with mischief, and then there was nothing else for it, you said a quick prayer and jumped for it, instantly waist deep in the glaur, and if there weren't dead weans in it there had to be dead dogs at least, and live rats for sure, and it smelled even worse than you could have imagined once you were right up close to it, you felt it soaking straight into you, and it was all you could do to stop yourself from gagging, and Mack just smiling drunkenly at you, the two of you stood there, and then him suddenly scrunched down again to start his kiddie-on crawl, and then there's splashes on either side of you, and whoops and groans, the whipped intake of breath, and Waldo and Joe are in too, Nate and Nora's man, fuck knows what he made of it, still stood on the bank, and Nate, for fuck's sake ya tadgers, there's every disease known to man in there, and Fiona, a big sigh and a shake of the head, och Derek.

Mack with the head start but you didn't bother even pretending at a swimming stroke, and you were at the other bank in about two seconds flat, gagging again and trying not to think of the stuff your feet were hitting on the bottom, about to climb up the bank and claim your trophy and whoosh, you felt a hand grabbing your shoulder, pulling you back, and then another hand on your head, pushing you down, and you closed your mouth instantly, waiting for the wipeout and holding your breath, and someone's full weight on you pushing themselves up as they pushed you down, and Mack's voice, what else, sorry big man but that trophy's mine, and your foot slipped on the slimy bottom and you went right under, and when you came back up Joe and Waldo holding Mack himself under now, and Waldo losing his footing too in the process, the comical look of alarm on his face as he submerged, and then all of you grabbing each other, a total free-for-all, each of you riotous one second and then abruptly silent the next, mouth tight shut and holding your breath as your head hit the water, you didn't dare swallow anything, and even one mouthful of the stuff would kill you for sure. And somehow in the confusion of it you managed to scramble out ahead of the others and then Mack in his best David Coleman voice, it's all about silver and bronze now, and Joe and Waldo jumping on him, one from each side, and the last word sounding more like nurrghud, and at last the three of them scrambling up to you on the pathway and Mack insisting on a medal ceremony right there and then on the Nolly bank, all of you stood shivering and hoaching, green slime clinging to your hair and your clothes, and of course Mack calling on Gillian to make the presentation of the trophy to you, her holding the manky thing out at arm's length in front of her as she handed it over to you and Mack making you cradle it close on your chest for the official photie, and that was fine, you were even more bowfing and manky than the trophy was, and at least you got a kiss on the cheek from Gillian, she was taking her life in her hands herself just doing that much, and fuck all medals or trophy for Joe and Waldo for silver and bronze, but fair play to Gillian, a kiss for each of them too, and both of them making to grab her for extras, but Gillian too quick for them, some wee drops of the glaur splashing on her good dress but she didn't seem to notice or mind, and Joe's lumber laughing and even Fiona taking it all in good part.

Then back to your house as quickly as you could go, the hurried goodbyes to the rest of them at the top of the road, and the arrangement was for Gillian to sleep in Louise's room, and Louise happy to stay up in the town with her pals from the Uni, she did it most weekends anyway, your mum and dad in bed already, it was after three, and you had to get straight up and into a hot shower, all your clothes and even your shoes destined for a binbag, and probably for the bin as well, you'd have to take a closer look in the morning, and Gillian, I'll just get up into my bed Andy, I don't want to disturb your mum and dad, another quick kiss on the cheek, holding her body and her good dress as far away from you as she could, and you didn't blame her for that, you could smell how gowping you were yourself, but when you came out of the bathroom you saw the strip of light at the base of the door, Gillian still up and awake in Louise's room, and you didn't know what it signalled, and maybe nothing, you thought about risking at least a wee chap on the door, but she'd already said goodnight, you should definitely respect that, and you went into your own wee totie room, and turned the lamp on and tried to read, and you knew you were waiting for something and hoping for something, you didn't even dare to name for yourself what.

And then hearing a door creak open and footsteps going into the bathroom, taps running, lavvy flushing, and all your senses fully alive, and the soft, careful footsteps again, waiting to hear where they would stop, and hoping with all your heart that they wouldn't stop but would keep coming, and then the door opening, and Gillian standing in the doorway, just a Rock Against Racism tee-shirt on, and you couldn't help it, your eyes went straight to her bare thighs, her legs lithe and bonnie like the rest of her, and you saw that she was blinking from the light of the lamp at your bed, and bright it would be coming from the darkness of the landing, and holding her finger to her lips for you both to be quiet, grimacing, pointing at the light, and you reached over to click it out, and she took a step and reached for it too, and you saw the flash of white scanties under the tee shirt, and she came over and sat on the bed, you sat up yourself and scootched over to make room, and she whispered she could only stay a couple of minutes, we don't want your mum and dad waking up and finding me here, and then you were kissing and the two of you lying on the bed together on top of the covers in the dark, and you never knew your bed creaked so much, every creak so loud it seemed like the bed was wired for sound, and the two of you half-giggling every time but not stopping, and everywhere you touched on her was soft, everything a curve, and you loved touching her, and her touching you, and you felt the breath catch in her throat, and she whispered again to you, did you have something, and you could hardly believe that you didn't, and straight into your head, the last thing you wanted to think about, big daft Porter, and his old man with the same routine, so he claimed, every time he went to a party, got yer booze, got yer fags, got yer johnnies, and then the nights, there were more than a few, sitting in the back of a brief while Joe or Waldo or Mack went haring round a tour of the local pubs trying to find a Durex machine that was loaded and working, and brandishing the packet triumphantly whenever they finally got one, and you didn't even know if you'd assumed that Gillian would be on the Pill or more likely that you just hadn't wanted to jinx yourself with stupid false hopes, and you whispered sorry, and fuck, and Gillian whispered that's okay, there's plenty time, and your heart soared at that more than anything else she could have said, and she said I need to get back through anyway, I don't want your mum and dad to know what a dirty stop-out I am, and you said yes, but now I know, and you pulled her back to you, and it was a good while yet before she finally pulled away, she held both your hands lightly as you let her go, and when she opened the door there was a wee bit of light from the landing, the day just beginning and the street light still on too through the thin curtains, and your eyes used to the dark now anyway, and the flash of white scanties again as she leaned to close the door, and almost as soon as she was gone you did what you had to do and came in about two seconds flat, and still you couldn't believe you would ever get to sleep, and next thing you knew it was morning.

8

Already into Sunday evening when you drove Gillian back to her flat in the town, she was changed now into her old jeans and a Bob Marley tee-shirt, and that was faded too, the round bit at the neck starting to fray and come away from the rest of the shirt, and she looked wonderful in a different way from last night, her hair tousled and her beautiful kind eyes still bleary and tired, pulling into Bellingham Terrace, and this time you went up the path with her into the graceful sandstone tenement and fuck, it turned out she wasn't kidding about the squalor, you really could hardly believe it, and she saw the look of shock on your face and laughed sheepishly, she must have been waiting for it. The whole thing just one person's house once in the days of the tobacco barons, and now in multiple occupancy for students, except that Gillian was the only actual student in the place you found out later, all the rest of them ex-students and drop-outs and lefties of one kind or another, the landlord had stopped maintaining the place and they were all withholding rent in protest, and Gillian admitting she'd never paid any in the whole six months she'd been there.

The big hallway with the stair in it telling you all you needed to know right away, the paint peeling off the walls and anyway stained and filthy from the smoke of smeegs and fuck knew what all, the carpet loose and bumphled up, whole patches of it black where the weave was gone, and the big bearded bastard the moment you opened the door, you found out later it was Nils the Viking, hammering away at some wooden thing he was building and Gillian, how's it coming there Nils, and the Viking, I've got the pillory done and I just need to get the stocks here finished, Gillian ending herself at your face as you climbed the stairs, and whispering to you that he had a big huge wooden cross too, eight foot at least, and every Easter he dragged it to Byres Road and back, and no-one could ever get him to explain exactly why. Glancing into the rooms on each landing as you walked past, most of the doors lying open, and you tried to keep the look of horror off your dial, one room with nothing in it but junk, piled high to the ceiling, and debris littered about, Kentucky Fried Chicken boxes and fish supper papers and fuck knew what, Gillian said some of the guys had started using it as a midden, and there had to be rats in there for sure, and when her dad had taken it on himself to call by unannounced not long after she moved in, and the place not even as bad then, he'd taken one look and said you need to sort yourself out lady and left, and you had to admit that you could kind of see where he was coming from, and Gillian, aye we'll see if you still say that when you meet him, and for some reason a wee thrill of pure pleasure went through you at that, and you said okay, you would see then.

Finally up to the third floor, that was where the big living room was, the smoke and smell of dope nearly choking you as you went in, and at first you thought it must be a party but Gillian said no, it wasn't unusual for a Sunday night, everyone saying hi Gillian when you came in, and hi Andy when she introduced you, and she found you both a space on the floor to sit, you were next to a big guy sitting cross-legged and taking a long drag of the joint that was going round, a beard on him, what else, and John Lennon specs too, and you thought fuck, here we go, but what a decent big guy, he was an anarchist he said, and you might have embarrassed yourself telling him what your mum always said but for Gillian mentioning on your first date that there were some anarchists sharing her flat and when you told her that was what your mum called you, she laughed and said you're no anarchist Andy and when you asked her what she thought you were then she laughed again but then looked earnestly right into your eyes and said do you really not know Andy, you're a romantic, and you hardly knew why it pleased you so, you were just glad there was no Mack or Joe or Nate around to hear her. And this guy Graham instantly as friendly as the wolf and delighted when he heard you were into punk, he had a Crass record he wanted to give you a tape of, and you had to follow him straight up a floor to his room so he could get it for you before he was too wasted to mind of it, and his room was at least not the worst of them, all manner of stuff tacked up on his walls, and one poster that you liked best, he was pleased when you told him and he said he'd made it himself, a full-page ad for wholemeal bread or real butter or something, a guy in a bunnet trailing a hand-held plough behind a big muckle Clydesdale, the two of them miserable and knackered-looking, and at the top where it should have said must be about time for my piece and real butter or whatever, Graham had put must be about time for us to smash the fucking state, the last four words in big huge capitals, and then insisting on playing you his favourite song off the tape right there and then on his tinny wee cassette player, they owe us a living, course they do, course they do, they owe us a living, course they fucking do, playing a wee imaginary drum kit to himself as you listened, and you didn't really think you would play it yourself, but it was kind of the guy, you tried to look enthusiastic and said great, and thanks very much.

And when you got back to the living room with your tape, Gillian already deep in an ardent discussion with the guys next to her, and you could tell it was high stuff, whether there was any point in reformism or if you should just wait for the revolution, Gillian arguing for the Labour Party and what was needed was organisation not talk, and Graham rolled his eyes at you and said what was needed was more bevvy and more laughs and more drugs, and Gillian told you later he was famous for the drugs, there was nothing he hadn't taken, and delighted that day because he just scored some amyl nitrate, if you could smoke it or swallow it or stick it up your arse big Graham was your man. And Graham telling you now that he was kicked out of Uni a year ago for failing all his exams, and in the question asking about Paul's letter to the Corinthians in Ecclesiastical History he'd just put lost in the post I'm afraid, and when you laughed and said was that not right then, he shook his head sadly, fuckers have no sense of humour. Anyway, he still haunted the QM bar, he knew a million folk that would sign him in, and he never missed any of the promotional nights with the cut-price bevvy, just a pity that it was always fucking bourgeois drinks, I'm a Buckfast man myself Andy, and he recited a poem he'd sent in to the QM Board, Bacardi's good, Pernod's fine, but give the punters Buckfast wine, but no-one on the Board was talking to him anyway he said, a bunch of them in the flat had liberated the wooden clothes poles from the QM compound to hang their black flags on, and he sang you a wee song for that too, the people's flag is deepest black, they'll never get their clothes poles back. And then some guys across the room heard that and they came in with oh my Stalin party line, and so high you can't get over it, so deep you can't get under it, so wide you can't get around it, that's the Berlin Wall, and they said the trouble with student politics was the fucking tankies, they were worse than the Tories, and it turned out they were anarchists too, and maybe you weren't an anarchist, and actually you were sure you weren't, but you liked every single one you'd met so far, the guys who were singing coming over to join you now and they were all just back from the weekend at a bothy in Bridge of Orchy, and they said they'd managed to partially smash the state there and they'd liberated the odd item for the use of the punters, and someone somewhere shouted whose turn was it to skin up, and one of the guys you were talking to took the pouch and the skins and the wee daud of brown stuff and started rolling the next joint, they were all experts at it so it seemed, and you took a draw when they offered it to you, you weren't a smoker but you managed not to embarrass your mother, and you got a wee hit from it you thought, watching their rituals and listening to their stories, and it occurred to you that there were teams everywhere, and all with their team histories, a thousand hearts, and Graham telling how a bunch of them had got drunk on tequila and one guy passed out and it seemed like a good idea to shave half the poor guy's hair off, the guy so out of it that he never woke up, and in the morning the guy on and on about how he had a job interview and calling them for everything, it was about to get ugly till Nils held a knife to the guy's throat and told him to calm down, which only proved that Nils had his uses, and wasn't just a total fucking psychopath, although he was mainly that, and no arguments from anybody.

And always the warm happy feeling inside you that you were there with Gillian, and memories of last night, catching her eye every so often, she was still solving the problems of the world over there, and her smiling at you, and you saw why the squalor didn't matter to her, and why she liked these people, and she looked pleased to see you liking them too, and you thought that maybe she was feeling at least a wee bit of how you felt when she pogoed with the team and endorsed the Canal Olympics, it felt good to have your mates approved of, and maybe you would try to explain that to her dad if you ever did meet him, you were feeling like you could do it right at this moment, but maybe the dope had affected you a wee bit more than you thought. The guys around you heavily into it now, Kropotkin and mutual aid and how Bakunin told Marx at the First International where it would all go, a Red Bureaucracy, beating the people with the people's stick, and ordinary folk tyrannized the same as before, and you followed most of it, it was fascinating actually, and then big Graham off into some random bullshit, he reminded you of Waldo, my hovercraft is full of eels, and frog for my tea, and feed your head the dormouse said, and you looked at your watch and saw it was after midnight, you'd only meant to stay half an hour, telling the guys you'd better get going but they hardly noticed you now, off in their own wee world, and Gillian saw you get up, and extricated herself too, and the two of you went up to her room, you were relieved when it was clean if not exactly tidy, she'd even put some emulsion on the walls, and a guitar in the corner, you never even knew she played the guitar, and a quick winch, you were both knackered and with work in the morning, and she wanted to give you a tape too, and she said you should try listening to some real music, but with a warm smile on her face, not meaning it really, you knew she just wanted to share it with you, and you took it gladly, and as soon as you hit the fresh air outside you felt your head spinning and you had to stand for a second or two before you got into the brief.

Driving back to Kirkie and the light was magical, the sky a deep rich blue and never fully dark at this time of the year, trying to concentrate on Gillian's tape, but your mind with its own ideas, the solemn way they all passed the joint around, and everyone considerate, careful not to hold onto it too long, respectful of that though just about fuck all else, you thought about the team, and you hardly ever saw Barney any more, he'd been fully signed on at one time and a decent guy, but never crashing the smeegs, always in the bogs when it was his round, and that stuff was important, all the rest of you super-careful to get your round in as soon as you saw any team glass close to empty, and you regularly with two or three full pints in front of you, hoping to catch up later when things slowed down, no point in even suggesting you could miss out a round, and often enough you had to switch to shorts for a bit, voddie and grapefruit to kill the taste of the voddie, you could get that down in a couple of quick gulps and maybe get back on track. And Nate would crash the smeegs religiously even when he only had a couple of singles, going into old Willie Fraser's with him on the way home from school, and old Willie would let you rummage through the wee wooden box of singles, and always a wee paper poke and a free book of matches for Nate, one of his best customers, Nate howking around for a Marlboro or an Embassy red, your mum and dad smoked them but they called them Embassy tipped, and only when you started hanging around with Nate did you even think about what tipped meant, saying it since you were just a wee kid at the shops and the ice cream van, twenty

Embassy Tipped please, you thought the tipped was just part of the name like the Embassy, Nate with his good grades and his school uniform incongruous round at the smokers but he could always do whatever he wanted, no-one messed with him and it came from inside him somewhere, the wee guys crowding round him, I'm on your dout big man, and Waldo, when he took a lend of his old man's pipe, and him and Mack round at the smokers, thinking they were the whole cheese, out with their pipe and their baccy, and when the jannie came and everyone else just ran for it, them stood with their wee pouch and their smouldering pipe, and the jannie could hardly keep a straight face marching them down to big Taylor's office.

Half way home before you pulled yourself together, and you'd half-heard most of it, you knew it wasn't for you, mostly mournful stuff that you didn't recognize, but then Bob Marley, and that was surprisingly good, one you hadn't heard before, we're coming in from the cold, Nate always saying that when the reggae came on at a party it was time to go home, and Leonard Cohen, you were all set to cut your wrists but actually that was good too, and even gave you a shiver, the couple touching each other's bodies with just their minds, and Simon and Garfunkel of all things, your mum and dad had their Greatest Hits, but this one could have been written just for you, he gets all the news he needs on the weather report, even singing along with it, and then stopped dead in your tracks, a man and a woman singing together, the intimacy and honesty of it so raw it was almost unbearable, her voice weaving in and out behind his and then wrapping around it, an impossibly perfect union, and you knew the song from the Nazareth version that had been in the charts, but this was off somewhere else altogether, all the fine things folk said about love, it was just for fools, but the man not fooled, he knew it wasn't true, the pain in his voice, and in the woman's voice too, so pure and sweet and truthful, you had to grab the box up off the seat and find out who it was, Gram Parsons and Emmylou Harris, the saddest thing you ever heard and yet somehow you could just let the sublime beauty of it wash over you and experience it for what it was, you were too happy for the sadness to touch you.

9

But still plenty work to do, and as the days went by a restless urgency underneath the happiness, Gillian asking you brightly when she was coming to Dunallan to watch you surf, and you were hardly less eager yourself, but still the bonds to be respected, the vows to be honoured, the backside turn still to learn and then the cutbacks, frontside and backside, an obligation owed to yourself and to the love and fellowship that was inside you to be dutiful and ready to face it when it came. And still always the feeling too that you were in a race despite yourself, that the time couldn't come too soon, and that there was something just beyond the horizon, something at stake that you couldn't quite bring into your vision or into your mind, however far you looked, however much you thought.

And still again the immediate joy, the blue sky roofing the calm abode of the landscape, the big left-breaks peeling from the promontory, and a good set visible again in the distance, and it was time to put all of that out of your mind and to concentrate, to find out exactly where you were after these days of diligent effort, and more wipeouts on this backside turn than in every other session put together, you had the scrapes and bruises to prove it, and only right in a way that they would come on your first point break, the sharp rocky bottom here a strict disciplinarian and not half as indulgent as the soft sand on the beach breaks, and now the time to bend your whole mind to the task if ever there was such a time, and yet still you knew your soul was strangely discordant. Half your nights spent at Gillian's these last couple of weeks, and you loved that part of it, but something troubling in the late night conversations with big Graham, and even the ones with your mum, she loved Gillian, and forever offering her drink, when did she ever do that for any of the team, tea good enough for them, and maybe a biscuit or a slice of toast if it was late, but not for the bold girl, would you like to try a gin and It Gillian, your mum's own drink, and Gillian pleased to try it, her nature as obliging and sweet as always, and she could hold it too, but even she said the ones your mum poured would blast your head off, you and your dad on a dispensation apparently, your mum never offered you drink either, and now both of you sat there quite the thing with your tins of your dad's Tennents from the fridge.

And the two females straight into it, you and your dad just spectators more or less, and your dad when he could get a word in much more interested in Gillian's law course than in politics anyway, telling her he always felt the lack of a degree himself, the ones at the College with the degrees always in there for the promotions and the cushy jobs, and it was one reason he wanted that for you and Louise, and so proud of Louise for breezing through all her exams at medical school, Gillian smiling and admitting, yes, she'd scraped through her First Year somehow, even Contracts that half the Year always failed, and that was a miracle, she had no idea how she'd done it, and your dad, ach she was just being modest, he knew a smart lassie when he saw one, and you even thought you saw a trace of the pride he always had in his eyes for Louise shining there now for Gillian.

But she hardly had the chance to reply, or even notice, your mum already deep back into it, wanting to know all the details of what was going on in the Labour Party, and Gillian just as keen to tell her, deefying the summer job her dad set up for her without a second thought, let the lawyers get their own bloody tea, and working instead for this mobilizing committee, and expected to co-ordinate the whole of Glasgow on her tod. Telling your mum that the Party was going to be different now, the loss at the election and even Thatcher herself maybe yet the best thing that could have happened, activists in the Party finally ready to make a fight, the resolutions passed at Conference never to be ignored again, the mobilizing committee was all set up, and all the groups on the left committed to working together for once. And it went beyond that, Tony Benn talking about bringing everyone in, not just the unions but the women's movement, Friends of the Earth, CND, the Anti-Nazi-League, the people protesting at Torness and Faslane, and against the cruise missiles that were coming to Greenham Common, but still right now nothing more urgent than the fight for the soul of the Party, there would never be a better chance for the grassroots to take control and build a true socialist movement, and the same thing in the unions, democracy now from the ground up, an electoral college to elect the leader and not just the PLP, right wing shower that they were, and mandatory reselection of MPs, no more jobs for life, and your mum cheered, there were plenty of MPs around here that could stand to go, they knew that people would vote for a donkey in Glasgow if you put a Labour badge on it, and a donkey more use than half of them, and why she would never join the Labour Party herself, but all this sounded great, and asking what she could do in the union to help.

Gillian saying that the Party itself would write the manifesto now and not Callaghan or his right wing cronies, and the resolutions already going in for Conference, all the things people wanted for years, and threatened or bribed into shutting up about them for the sake of keeping power, unilateral nuclear disarmament, and public ownership and out of the Common Market, and even your dad came in with an aye, quite right, bloody capitalists' club, and Benn set to run for leader, and he could win, Thatcher so unpopular, so bent on destroying the unions she didn't care about anything else, it was coming back to bite her, and Gillian with all the facts at her fingertips, unemployment up again, and that was a given for all their cynical talk before the election about Labour wasn't working, but much more important for them trade exports and retail sales down, and capital investment too, even some of their fat-cat pals in the City starting to waver, and the wets in Thatcher's own Party nervous, ready to bail out on her, there would never be a better time to get a foot in the door for socialism. Gillian taking a gulp of your mum's firewater, and trying to get her breath back, and you saw that your mum was caught up in it all too, overjoyed that you met someone like Gillian, and you knew what she was thinking, how great it would be if you could be working too for something so worthwhile, and making something out of your life the way Gillian was.

And in a way you were grateful for big Graham, inviting himself into Gillian's room with you, and making himself at home, and dismissing it all with a drunken smile, swigging on his tumbler of the Buckie, and where do you think your precious Tony Benn was while Callaghan and the rest of them were fucking us all over in the first place, and Gillian starting in, I know, but Graham not waiting for her, I'll tell you where, serving in Callaghan's Government, that's where, fucking us all over with the rest of them. Graham smecking away to himself at the joke of it, and Gillian, unfazed, saying that was the whole point, and Tony made no bones about it himself, it was all in Arguments For Socialism, no individual could overcome the power structures, that's what his experience taught him, that's why he didn't stand for the Shadow Cabinet, that's why we needed to change the structures, and you saw her warming to it again, the point is he's with us now, and Graham, oh right, he's with us now is he, would that be now that he's out on his arse with the rest of them by any chance, and Gillian still fired up, it wasn't about Tony Benn anyway, it was about changing the structure of the Party, so that whoever was put in there had to do what the grassroots told them, and if they buckled to the Establishment they'd be gone, de-selected or brought back into line.

And Graham nearly choking on his Buckie at that one, but he just said all right, suppose somehow you get all that, do you really think they'll just stand back, the Yanks and the rest, and say good luck to you then. Look at Cuba Gillian, look at Chile and Nicaragua, take a wee look at the flight of capital, the embargoes, the blockades, the bleeding you dry, and making you run to the fucking Union of Soviet Fucking Fascism to save your revolution or your wee democratic reforms. And by the way they won't stop short of a military coup here either if they have to, don't kid yourself that it couldn't happen, the slightest chance of all your pie-in-the-sky Mickey Mouse bullshit actually happening and they'll have the tanks back in George Square, and the two of us waiting to be tortured and disappeared at Hampden, and big Andy in with us as a fellow-traveller, and all he ever wanted was his nookie.

And Gillian with the riddie, but the fight still in her, not if we organize, not if we give the Party back to the people, the people will stand with us, and she was flying now, how the people wouldn't let it all be taken away, how once they saw them working they'd fight for the things they had, fight for public ownership, fight against the Common Market, against cruise missiles and Polaris and being a weapons dump for the US, the people would fight and the people would resist and the people would this and the people would that.

And into your head unbidden came the image of your Pop, making his own way back home through the East End streets, not even late yet and plenty of the people around, and his face cut and bleeding, and not a soul coming to his aid, him that would do anything for anyone, and within the year he was dead, and a heart attack so they said, but your Grandma would always talk about those ones that killed your Pop, and she said the doctors told her the beating he took at least contributed, there never was a stronger, more robust man until then, and your mum would always say no Mammie, that's not right, but somewhere inside yourself you always knew that it was right, that the people would do fuck all, the people would take everything you had to give and then the people would look after themselves, and the folk like your Pop and your mum and Gillian were wasted on the people and they should be doing what everyone else did, looking after themselves and their own, what was the point of being a martyr, and Gillian might as well lie herself down on Nils the Viking's big cross and let him drag her down to Byres Road as put her faith in the people to do anything.

But you didn't say that, you just let them talk, though you must have given some clue, because later in the bed, and the softness and warmth of it matching her own warmth and her own softness, Gillian said I'm really committed to this Andy, I won't give it up for anything you know, and you said of course not and that you thought it was great and that you were on the side of the people too, though your own tendencies were anarchist as she knew, and she laughed, the sweet kind nature of her, and not much later you felt her fall asleep, still holding her, and wishing you didn't have to sleep yourself and you could just lie there awake like this all night and think about how much you loved her, and hope that the tightening you felt somewhere deep inside you was nothing, just the fears anyone would have about losing something so precious, no other reason for it but your own contrary nature, and your mum and dad always saying you had to be worrying about something.

And all of it instantly gone anyway the moment you and Gillian hooked up with the team, and right away then you truly didn't worry, and you couldn't even think why you ever would, and as if Mack had appointed himself Social Convenor for Gillian's amusement, the game of cricket down the Waterside park, and Gillian sitting the whole game in the glorious sunshine watching idly and chatting away easily with the other lassies, though you knew yourself she'd rather be playing. Joe and yourself down to Harry Benson's before you started for the rolls and bacon, and Joe buying a bottle of Vimto, taking a big gulp on his way back to the brief, and then you saw it come spraying straight back out again, Harry's home-brew red wine in the bottle instead of the scoosh, and intended only for his more select customers, but the bottles mixed up somehow behind the counter, and when you got back to the park Nate claiming Harry had used snake in the rolls instead of bacon, and he had a point, the stuff was all stringy and curled up, and in the end even Joe gave up on it, howked a daud of it out of his roll and threw it to a place of fuck. And when the game finally got started thank fuck none of you knew how to bowl properly or you'd have killed yourselves, the big hard cricket ball coming at you faster than you would have believed was possible, even useless as you all were at lobbing the thing, and the only other gear you had was the wooden stumps and the bats and a pair of old leather gloves Allie came up with for the wicket-keeper. Nate with the idea of everybody fielding given the low numbers you had, and Mack with the easy catches mysteriously dropped whenever his side were batting, then Nate and Allie coming together for a heroic last wicket stand, and when Nate sconed one and they crossed in the middle, him peching and wheezing from the smeegs, just take the one Allie, I'm fannied. And still Nate protesting to the imaginary umpire about the daud of bacon on the wicket so he claimed, it was affecting the bounce of the ball, and when he was finally out at last walking back over to where the lassies were sat, and muttering that was snake before wicket, that was fucking sbw.

And then everybody back to the Vale, all the rest of them stiff and sore already, hirpling about like old men, and you pretended to be crocked too though you saw Mack looking suspiciously at you, arrangements to be made for the inaugural Merkland Open putting tourney next weekend, all of you to come up with the names of the holes to commemorate famous events in team history, and then in the tourney itself Mack convinced apparently that the names were in some kind of secret impenetrable code, yelling at the top of his lungs to all of you, scattered about the big field of a putting green, Pohl just took ten at The Messy Settee, Pohl drops out of contention at Drumshanty Drop, Pohl fails to read the break at She Didnae Half, the wee kids smirking and their parents scowling over at him, and Dan Pohl the name he chose for himself, Allie was John Panton of Glenbervie, and Nate was Hubie Green, the only golfer who was worth a fuck so he claimed, he seemed to know something about it as usual though you knew he had no real time for the golf, watching the US Masters last year at Allie's and when the big gormless guy holed out on the eighteenth and his wee wife ran on to give him a hug, that's the Krankies, that's the fucking Krankies by the way. But everybody had to have a name, and Gillian insisting on playing this time, she got Christy O'Connor Junior, Waldo was Artie McNickle, Nora's man was Gaylord Burrows, and you were Nick Job, and then the perplexed look on Fiona's face when she was pulling the names for the tee-times out of Joe's baseball hat, and she pulled out yours, and she stood there frowning at it, nick-job, what's a nick-job, laughing herself as she saw you all crack up, and refusing to believe you even when you told her he was a real golfer like the rest, and the surname pronounced like the guy in the Bible, and still Fiona, no but seriously, what's a nick-job, what's a nick-job.

Back in the Vale after the team photie for the archives, all the families in for their Sunday bar lunches, and nothing to beat the prospect of a slow, lazy all-day session, Joe with the story of how him and Mack had been out cruising last week and spotted a total honey, Mack rolling down the window to tell her to get her panties off, and Joe putting the guttie down just to mess with his timing, Mack had to try and get the words out extra quick before they were past her, and the only word that made it out of his mouth was pants, and Joe swore he could see the lassie in the mirror looking after them and wondering who was the sad bastard shouting pants at her, he couldn't even get his sexual harassment right. But Mack straight back at him, what about the time before that then, Joe riding shotgun in the Bendy Buggy and they saw Kathy Calderwood up ahead on the pavement, and then it was Joe rolling down the window and dropping his breeks to hang his big bare arse out at her, and what he thought that was supposed to achieve Mack had no idea. And then the mischievous wee glint in his eye, though actually, he says, I did bump into her the other day and she did mention you, and Joe walking right into it, he couldn't help himself, everybody fancied Kathy Calderwood, really, what did she say, and Mack, she said he's got awful wee balls, hasn't he.

Gillian hooting with the rest of you, her hand up to her mouth, you could tell she was trying her best not to, and what would all her feminist pals say if they witnessed that display. Wading back to Allie's for canasta when the Vale finally closed, everybody out of their box and on a high, and an old drunk guy staggering around a full hundred yards ahead of you, and Joe, if that's Nick Porter I'm going to boot his arse, all of you rolling at that one, the guy was about ninety and nothing like big Porter, and Joe scowling at you, he truly didn't see what was funny about it. And then at the canasta, the standard team speak, and none of you even thought about it now, telling each other you were dropping the scants when you made the fifty points and were ready to lay down, and when you hit your card you banged your hand down triumphantly and told everybody to take it in the mouth, and then you thought fuck, and you looked across at Gillian, and you saw she was laughing, her face softer and kinder than ever from the bev, and you felt like your heart might burst from the joy of it.

And now it was you tiptoeing softly into Louise's room, Gillian waiting for you, and just a cuddle anyway the night, on holiday yourself but Gillian with work in the morning, and you driving her, and a treat to do it, to spend that time with her, and all your fears about your performance in the sack seeming a distant memory already, Gillian knowing surely that your first time in her flat with her was your first time ever, but she never asked, and you never asked how she knew what she knew, still guiding you so tactfully, oh that's nice Andy, or gently Andy, even taking your hand to show you, or taking hold of you to guide you, and asking you what was nice for you, and all you could say was that everything was nice, the softness and the warmth of her, the gracefulness in everything she did, and even now it was all you could do in fact to keep it to a cuddle, right there in the strangeness of your sister's room, and tired and drunk and sated as you were.

The thought of that finally enough so it seemed to break you from the bondage of your false thoughts and false philosophies, a secret happiness spreading through you once again, and you were ready for the high privilege that lay before you, your wave looming in the near distance, and you could see it would be fully head height when it reached the lineup, paddling as fast as you could and then it was on you, and you were taking off straight down the face, knees bent and leaning into the turn, your weight on the tail and the inside rail of your board, all of it practically an instinct too, and all the hard work was to make it that, but now the true test, so many times before with too much weight on the inside, stalling, unable to stay on the clean face of the wave, the long painful wipeouts in the washing machine of the surf and the punishing dance with the sharp rocks on the bottom, and then fucking up the other way, too little weight on the rail, the tail too light, and the board failing to make it round the turn before the lip came crashing down on top of you, another wipeout and more of the same, and it was fair and just, you deserved it and you bore it, but you wanted to be past it, and all at once you saw that you were now, your feet planted firm and parallel on the board, your weight angled back to the face, and your back to the wave, and the turn made smoothly, easily, and on a head-high wave, and now you just glided along the clean, fast-rushing face of it, you knew it was peeling behind you though you couldn't see it, and this your just reward for all you'd given to it, the sea and the swells and the waves not cruel like was sometimes said but only stern and just, and generous now, sharing with you everything they themselves had to give, and the backside turn learned at last.

10

Gillian saying she fancied the film at the GFT, and you said fine, the big curved screen and the ushers showing people to their seats with their wee torches, a throwback to how the pictures were when you were a kid, except that here the ushers weren't mature women but students from the Uni by the look of them, and guys and lassies both doing it, huddling together and whispering to each other in the aisles when the film started, and no kiosk for sweeties or ice-cream or any of the usual stuff, the place quiet and respectful, everyone there to give their full attention to the picture, a lot of students in the audience too, and the team always deefied the place for exactly those reasons even when they had a good film on, but you liked it, you'd been with your mum and dad and Louise a bunch of times over the years, and glad when Gillian suggested going there.

And it was All That Jazz you were seeing, the wee usher guy handing you a typed sheet with information about the picture on it, and you liked that too, and you read that the guy who had directed this one also directed Cabaret, and straight into your head the demo at Faslane, Gillian asking if you wanted to go, and of course you didn't, you just wanted to be with Gillian, and you said great, marching behind the Glasgow Uni CND banner, and Gillian, bright and vivacious, and bantering with everyone, the obvious empathy she had with people, taking the tray of Books Not Bombs badges that no other fucker could sell, and they were all gone in no time, and ach just keep the change dear, it's great to see the young people out, and it was like the dancing, you could see the fun in it if you were like that and could do it, but when you weren't like that the whole day was torture, you never felt more isolated and lonely and miserable than standing in the big crowd, listening to the inspiring speeches, and all the music and jollity and exuberance seemed forced to you, as if you had to show anyone watching what fun people you were really, and how you knew how to have a good time even if you were earnest and sincere and caring, the tables of tasteless organic food, everything needing salt, and the kids with balloons and their faces painted, and the badges, I want to grow up, not blow up, and if it's so bloody safe put it under Westminster, the wee knot of guys all in black with their weird sinister placards, they were Spartacists Gillian said, and in favour of the Workers' Bomb apparently, and the SWP, Gillian said they were always at everything, over and over the whole time, Maggie Maggie Maggie Out Out Out, and from somewhere else behind you, och och get out the Holy Loch, and the only one that cheered you up out of all of them was the strange-looking guy muttering to himself and with his own homemade sign, nuclear weapons fuck off.

You knew you didn't feel the way you were supposed to feel, and you even knew it was ridiculous in such a benign good-natured gathering, and half the people with white hair and needing sticks to get them through the length of the march, but you couldn't help it, you still felt a kind of quiet panic at what any crowd might do at any time, and you said nothing then and just tried your best not to let Gillian down, but now seeing the mention of Cabaret in the sheet, and Gillian reading it too, for some reason you started talking to her about it, all the films with the swelling music when a big mob stood shoulder to shoulder, and yes Humphrey Bogart or Tony Curtis or whoever was honourable and noble, and maybe even the one or two that would come in after them, but everybody else was surely just jumping on the bandwagon, seeing the main chance, and the opportunity there to bully whoever was in the minority now, and Gillian looking at you puzzled,

Tony Curtis, you mean I am Spartacus, and you said yes, and what you meant was that when his character said he was Spartacus, and the guy a few yards away straight in to say it as well, fair enough that was genuinely moving, but weren't all the other guys just following the crowd, and Gillian said what, following the crowd to be crucified you mean, and she had a point you had to admit but you knew what you meant, a lot of films like that, people acting together, it was supposed to inspire you, but it always did the opposite for you, and the only film you ever saw that showed the truth of it you thought was Cabaret, the scene with the wee blonde Hitler Youth singing Tomorrow Belongs To Me, apathy at first and then a wee bit of interest and then the music swells and one after the other they all get up to their feet and sing, and the thing is you do feel something, it does stir something up in you, you can't help it, and the guy Fosse brave enough to show that, all the adults standing up with their big beer mugs and singing their heads off, a triumph of the human spirit and everyone in solidarity, and the only problem is that they're Nazis, the wee old guy sat despairing and shaking his head, he knew what it really meant, and you thought that you did too.

And Gillian looking thoughtfully at you, and maybe she would have said something back, but right then the lights went down and the curtain went back, and just like that, the film was on, no ads or trailers or anything, another big difference about the GFT, and as it turned out, All That Jazz was a totally different kind of film from Cabaret anyway, the guy a choreographer and with a big sign saying Oh Wow on his wall, you loved that, and the incredible talent he had, cheating on all his women, and his girlfriend as talented as he was, a brilliant dancer, and onto him for screwing around, and him, the big chancer of him, telling her he's trying to give all he can give, and her reply to him, I just wish you weren't so generous with your cock. And the best scene when the girlfriend and the guy's wee daughter come dancing down the stairs of his apartment, a special routine they've come up with just to cheer him up, he's such a tortured artist, the two of them each with both hands on the banister for support, one behind the other, and jumping their way down the steps in time to the music, and the song they dance to, everything old is new again, and you sat holding Gillian's hand, you knew she was loving the movie, and you were too, and the song going round in your head for the whole rest of the film, and the whole rest of the night, dreams coming true again, because everything old was new again.

And then Apocalypse Now, it seemed like such a happy combination, the GFT showing it and the rave review in NME, Francis Ford Coppola himself holding the NME up at a press conference and saying how this was the best article of all of the ones he'd seen, this guy McKinnon had really studied his film and understood what he was trying to do, and you actually felt a wee bit of reflected glory, you and Nate and Allie loyal NME readers from way back, and still doing lines from the big Christmas Quiz two years back, what did Ronnie Biggs sell for punk, his soul, his arse or his heavy metal records, and Angus McKinnon making Coppola's film seem like a real masterpiece, exactly Gillian's kind of thing, and only after you went to the moot at the Uni did you begin to understand properly why it had been such a disaster.

A moot something you'd never even heard of before, and Gillian trying to put you off coming at all, if she'd have known they'd get to the semi-final and be still having to do it in the summer she'd never even have gone in for the thing so she said, but once she explained to you what it was and that she was the main speaker for her side, there was nothing in the world was going to stop you being there to see her. And walking into the hall you felt a kind of intense secret pride, the place packed though she'd said there would probably be no-one there, taking a seat at the back and no-one in the whole room even knew that was your girlfriend up there, so cool and professional in her plain white blouse and black skirt, her hair tied back, arranging her books and papers and talking to her teammate, the two guys from the Edinburgh Uni team across on the other side of the table, and the lawyer who was acting as the judge sat up on the stage above them at his own table in his suit and tie. The two guys next to you in their Pringle jumpers, rugby players by the look of them, and when the compere guy introduced the teams and got to Gillian, and she stood up and gave her wee bow, both of them stamping like mental patients on the wooden floorboards, their big tree-trunk legs pumping, and a lot of others doing the same thing, that seemed to be how it was done, though there was some conventional applause too, and one saying to the other in a big loud voice, what would you not do to that, and you said hey and scowled at him, and all you could think was that either one of them could have papped your napper and hardly broken sweat, but they just scowled back at you and then shut up, maybe it was the Wrangler jacket, and the shameful truth was that you weren't even offended by what the guy said, you just felt even luckier and even prouder in your undercover way.

But what a nauseating thing it was to watch in fact, the two guys on before Gillian, her own teammate and the Edinburgh guy, straight up the judge guy's browner from the off, and whatever they had prepared obviously abandoned in the first few seconds, the judge guy interrupting each of them in turn to let them know what he thought himself about the case and then them repeating back to the fucker what he'd just said to them, as your Lordship points out, and if I could adopt your Lordship's reasoning, and yes, I'm very grateful to your Lordship, laughing like hyenas at the guy's terrible pompous jokes, and everyone seemingly in agreement that the case the Edinburgh side were arguing was the obvious winner, though you knew fine well from Gillian that the cases were supposed to be carefully thought up to make sure there were good points to be found on both sides. And then Gillian an absolute fucking star, showing the bastard total courtesy and politeness, he was up to his capers with her the same as with the others, and you could hear the nervousness in her voice at first, but she didn't bend over like they did, I must respectfully disagree my Lord, and then again and again through all his bad manners, if your Lordship would just bear with me, if your Lordship would just bear with me, warming to it and sticking to her guns and leading him through it, the fucker harrumphing and raising his eyebrows as she made him look at all the big volumes laid out on the table in front of him, and reading the apposite passages out loud to him anyway so he couldn't avoid it, and him rolling his eyes and interrupting her every two seconds, and more and more irritable and impatient the more she wouldn't take his points, making it obvious to everyone she was wasting his time.

And then the wonderful moment, and surely it was obvious to everyone in the place, when he suddenly saw it, and saw that she was right, and that he'd been off on the wrong track the whole time, and dragging everyone else with him, and it served them right the sycophantic bastards, and even then the pompous fucker couldn't resist saying it all back to her as if he'd just thought of it himself and maybe he'd have even thought of it sooner if she hadn't kept distracting him. But Gillian still the soul of tact and courtesy, yes my Lord and no my Lord, and with respect this and respectfully the other, and unless I can assist your Lordship further I'll conclude there, sitting down to another wee bout of the stamping and no doubt whatsoever that she had blown the other side's case right into the weeds. Sure enough, the final Edinburgh guy getting the usual two seconds before the judge guy is in on him, but now the fucker putting Gillian's case to the Edinburgh guy exactly as if that's what he'd been saying himself all along, and the best of it that this wee Edinburgh guy goes right along with that too, yes I can see my difficulty my Lord, and your Lordship makes a very good point, and would your Lordship like a wee rub of my balls by any chance, and now everybody seemingly in agreement that the case Glasgow were arguing had to be the winner and a shame really that brilliant minds like theirs should have to waste their time on something so obvious, and you sat there hardly able to believe the whole thing, but still the glow of your secret pride in Gillian, so calm and so poised and smiling politely now at everyone.

Finally the judge guy giving his verdict on the case, a win for the Glasgow side of course but, he says, and giving his big smug knowing grin, as if he's so far above these things that it wouldn't even occur to him unless someone told him, he's led to believe that the legal outcome isn't the most important thing on occasions such as this, and another big bout of stamping, the guys beside you giving it full laldy, and it was a very spirited performance by both teams, he says, but in the end one team just that bit more professional, conducting themselves just that bit more in accordance with the great traditions of the Bar, and you thought fuck, here it comes, and sure enough he gave it to the Edinburgh team, you waited for the riot, the crowd ripping the seats up and flinging them on stage like when Root Boy Slim got his knob out at the Apollo, his band the support act for The Police, waggling the thing around like a pervy old flasher, and The Police themselves lucky to get away without more of the same, Can't Stand Losing You played three times they had so few songs rehearsed, but anyway this crowd were at least more civilized thank fuck, you were cowering at the Apollo, still at school and your first ever concert there, and this lot applauding politely, the wee Edinburgh contingent stamping their feet off, and for all the world like no-one even noticed what just happened.

By the time you could get up there, the judge guy down from the stage and already talking to Gillian and her teammate, and another middle-aged guy, and you knew that must be Gillian's old man, prematurely grey, but handsome, the expensive suit and the aftershave, and he had a gold wedding ring and cufflinks on, and a whole air about him that he knew exactly what he was doing at all times, you could hear him and the judge guy helping Gillian out with where she went wrong in her presentation, and not a bit surprising when you looked at them that they would know each other and be old buddies, nodding distractedly at you for about a millisecond when Gillian saw you and tried to introduce you, and Gillian still with the fixed polite smile on her face, listening attentively to the two smug pompous fuckers that weren't fit to lick her boots, and it wasn't as if you'd had no clue about the Apocalypse Now thing before, it was just that now you felt it for the first time in your heart the way Gillian surely felt it, the rage and the despair and the feeling of utter helplessness, and you'd have given anything in that moment to be Joe, to just wade straight in without a second thought, and grab one of them, you didn't even care which, get him by the lapels of his fancy suit and pin him up against the wall, and just for that one second see the look of terror on both their smug pompous coupons, that was all you'd do you hoped, and it would be enough for you. But you weren't Joe, you didn't have his instinctive courage, and if you were thinking about it then you weren't doing it by definition, and you just stood there, pathetic and helpless, watching Gillian bear it all with her fixed polite smile, and how long had she been doing that, surely all the years of her life, waiting patiently for her old man to be done with the other fucker, he was supposed to be taking you both out for a drink, and his idea even, not hers or yours.

And through your mind the night at Apocalypse Now, the typed sheet from the usher, and noticing that the script for it was by the guy that did Big Wednesday, another good sign so it seemed. Sure enough a surfing sequence in the film, but by then you were hating the whole thing so much it was hard to judge, the surfing bombastic and hateful and mean-spirited like everything else on the screen, and you couldn't tell if it had been meant to be like that or just swallowed up by the confusion and malevolence that engulfed everything else. Gillian so quiet beside you that you assumed she was getting all the political significance that McKinnon had in his review, and you were determined to see it out to the end for her sake, and then, I'm sorry Andy, I just can't take any more of this, and she was down the stairs and out into the street before you could even catch her, and then you never saw anyone cry like that for people she didn't even know, another country and another race, thousands of miles away, and the bitter angry tears, and she said it wasn't anger it was shame, all the millions spent exploring our angst and what happened to us, and hardly a thought for what we did, millions tortured and killed, children still dying every day from our chemicals and poisons and landmines, and if you even tried to as much as point it out, you were hysterical and emotional and you needed to be more rational and objective, and the Vietnamese needing to be rational and objective too, and maybe apologise for all the angst they caused us, and we never even see it that it's us, it's rational, objective, patient, tolerant, reflective, benevolent, smug, self-satisfied us, we're the heart of darkness Andy, we're the heart of darkness, and you looked now at her old man and his buddy stood pontificating in their expensive suits and their aftershave and you saw that it was true, and you didn't need to be some big politician or civil servant to have those attitudes and to make sure all of it would always keep happening, you only needed to be a self-satisfied fucker of a Glasgow lawyer, a good family man, and bringing your kids up the right way, and you saw how Gillian had been born into it, and how she'd turned her back on it, and had gone her own way, and what must it have cost her, smiling politely now at this wee silly outrage because it didn't matter to her, saving her anger and her shame and her tears for the things that did matter, and the love and admiration you felt for her then, you knew it would be locked forever in your soul.

Finally away to the Curlers in Byres Road, Gillian's old man looking disdainfully around at the empty glasses and flattened crisp pokes on the tables, the couples smooching in the dark corners, and Gillian giving you a sly smile when he asked her what she was drinking these days, I'll have a gin and It please dad. And you were sure he would have to be curious about it, and you were all ready to tell him it was what your mum always gave his daughter at your warm, kind hospitable house, but fuck all chance of that, the old bastard muttering something to himself about her Communist pals and a good way of getting two drinks bought for you instead of one, and when he came back from the bar with the wee tray, presenting your bog standard pint of Tennents to you like you were homeless and he was the Salvation fucking Army, smacking his gums on his pathetic single measure of neat malt whisky like a wee old dear sooking tea out of a saucer, and you got your pint down somehow in three big gulps, trying to open your throat and pour it down like Joe or Mack would do if they fell behind from playing the spacies or chatting up Lynne or Janie, but you couldn't do it, your eyes watering from the gas and bubbles in the stuff, and wishing you liked the heavy better, it was definitely flatter and easier to gub down, but anyway straight up to the bar and your round in before

Gillian and her old man were even halfway down their drinks, and making sure that he got a double of his fancy single malt, whether he wanted it or not. The baffled look on the man's face when you asked why Mrs Harper couldn't make it the night, as if he just couldn't compute what the words might mean, and Gillian coming in to say that it wasn't really her mum's cup of tea, her old man straight back in to lecturing her about where she'd gone wrong, and the trouble she'd have been in if she took that approach in a real court with a real judge, and you couldn't help yourself, you said hadn't he seen that his pal was getting it all wrong and needing Gillian to put him right, and surely in a real case that was what lawyers were for, and the look the fucker gave you, as if the guy cleaning his lavvy had tried to give him tax advice or something, and you felt yourself instantly with the huge riddie, Gillian touching your knee under the table, and she said actually dad, we need to get going, Andy's mum and dad are expecting us in Kirkie, and you loved that, she knew fine well you were headed straight back to her flat and not the slightest intention of wading out to Kirkie, and you looked her dad straight in the eye, yes Mr Harper, they're throwing a wee party for Gillian, you heard her snorting into her drink and trying to pass it off as a coughing fit and she said, so is Jimmy Reid coming Andy, and you said aye you thought so, and maybe bringing Mick McGahey, and from the look of disgust on the fucker's face you weren't even sure whether he knew you were taking the piss or if he really thought you were telling the truth, or which one he would have thought was worse.

11

Back on the beach at Dunallan, the pensive sky and the healthful offshore breeze, and the strangeness in your mind lifted the moment you saw it, the sand on the floor shifted around so it seemed by the recent swells, and a new sandbar in the wee bay, the waves peeling left and right off it to either side, and just like that the opportunity there for all the cutbacks you could ever want, frontside and backside both, and as if the sea itself was whispering to you, the ghostly language of ancient earth, shaping the measure and prospect of your soul to its own majesty, drawing you back to universal things, to the never-failing principle of joy that first drew you here. Finding the lineup on the frontside, and it took a few tries, the right-breaks slightly unpredictable in this fresh configuration, but a small price to pay, and even the time you were caught inside the break you felt a tranquility spread itself through you undismayed, a calmness breathing too in the dark water itself, and you stayed down till you sensed the commotion above you ease, opening your eyes to watch for all the roil and bubble of it beginning to recede, and then you kicked quickly up to the surface, and you were out of the impact zone before the next one came crashing down, off to find your board and into the channel to the lineup.

Then making the drop on the wave and carving out the bottom turn in the trough, and that came easily now, powerful and clean, but when you tried for the cutback itself your turn too strong and you went back too far, you felt the white water rush up over the deck, and then you were caught, no possible way to make the next crucial turn back onto the shoulder, and you wiped out that time, and the next and the next, and failing so often in fact that you made rigorous inquisition through yourself, ready to face a chastening truth, and found instead that your faith in the nobility of the task before you was undiminished, your soul unsubdued, and you were ready to dedicate yourself again, and only to yield for a time your lofty hopes for present gifts of humbler industry. Trying for a gentler turn then, your weight shifted more gradually to the outside rail and the tail, but now it was too gradual, and you were too far out on the shoulder, stalling, your momentum gone, and with no chance to get the board all the way round and back to the pocket, and wiping out time after time again, not in the fizz and turbulence of the white water any more but peacefully now, and uselessly, stranded on the spent face of the dying wave.

And yet you knew that you were not to be withstood, that every failure of this day and of every previous day was an envoy of future success, and you had no impatient hopes or vain conceits or excessive zeal but just a quiet openness of mind, every fresh attempt bringing fresh access of knowledge, and the delight of knowledge, and matching the sea's own delight in its severe ministry, its joy in subjecting you to the discipline of love. And still it was late in the session when you had it at last, making the drop on the face, harnessing every last bit of the wave's speed and power, giving all you had of your own, a clean powerful turn in the trough, pushing the board as high as it would go on the face, and now the cutback, your weight on the outside rail, your head and body turned back towards the pocket and your back foot knowing finally what was needed, guiding your board round towards the white water, your back to the wave, and your arms knew their part too, and stretched out to help balance you, and just as you felt the board bounce on the white water you made the second turn, shifting your weight again, your back foot the pivot, and the water spraying out under the rail as you made the turn, frontside to the face again, and perfectly back in the pocket now, all of the wave's ferocious energy available to you all over again, and you could cut back as often as the wave had energy to give. And all of it right there before you, whole and complete the instant it was done, you could see it so clearly, and not from your eyes, and you almost forgot that you had eyes, but as something in yourself, a dream, a prospect in your mind.

Then finding the new lineup for the left-breaks, it was near but not quite the same, and truth be told you weren't even surprised when it came easily now, the backside usually so much harder than the frontside and yet you knew the sea was honouring the bond, recognising your trust in what you might become, and when you made the first turn on the backside you were facing the wave, and the difference it made, you could see the white water coming as you swept round to face the curl, and you let your back foot squeeze the pressure down onto the tail, and your weight so subtly and decisively over onto the outside rail, and just as the white water tried to swallow you up you leaned smoothly into the second turn, and then you were racing again fast along the face, you could do it all day and every day now, frontside or backside, the last barrier gone to direct and intimate communion with any wave, and nothing any longer to restrain the fusion of your energies, joining hope to your hope, love to your love.

And ready at last too for Gillian's visit to Dunallan, driving back along the M8, her tape playing on the stereo, and you'd played nothing else since she went down to Brighton, but the calmness in your mind still from the session, a cheerful confidence in the things to come, your thoughts on high objects and enduring things, and your fears under just and proper restraint, the first time since your first date that you hadn't seen her for anything more than a couple of days and of course you would miss her and of course you would worry about her, and all of it only the most natural and mundane thing in the world, a poor bastard lovesick and pining for his bird. Watching Callaghan on the news at the TUC Conference, you smiled at the thought of it, when would you ever have done that before, and how we have to be united in the fight against Thatcher, and we mustn't divide the Party, and we must resist those who would, and your mum, that's your Gillian he's talking about Andy, and she was right, it was Gillian, and all the other people involved with her Committee, down there now at the fervent, tumultuous heart of it, the phone calls and the meetings and the lobbying and the organizing, the unions worked on for their own sake but even more as a dress rehearsal for the Party Conference at the end of the month, and the excitement in her voice when she came on the phone, even Ireland was up for discussion now, the Young Socialists with a motion going to Conference about Long Kesh and the H-blocks, and Callaghan was trying to get it referred back and buried but the fight was on, and you remembered Nate telling you what they shouted on their Troops Out demos, H-block Hell-block Troops Out Now, the anguish and the pain of it so real to them and yet to you now it seemed so far away, and Gillian so far away, and the strangeness threatening to invade your thoughts again, and you turned away from it, and grateful that there was something else waiting, the encounter with Gillian's old man still thoroughly alive in your mind, and everything it stirred up inside of you, the things you always took for granted before that night, and how precious they seemed after it, how significant and charged with sudden meaning, and over and over in your head, everything old is new again.

The start of it still the delicious thought of Gillian telling the old fucker you were going back to Kirkie, and how it seemed to you then, and even more now, that your wee house in Spam Valley really was some kind of safe haven, a sanctuary of goodwill and ordinary human decency, unthinkable that your mum would miss anything like Gillian's moot if it was Louise doing it, and for that matter absolutely fuck all that wasn't her cup of tea where either of her kids was involved, or that wasn't your dad's cup of tea either, the two of them so silently and unobtrusively equal as partners that it never entered your head before that there could be any other way. Remembering their kindness to Gillian, and the way her old man treated you, and you felt a new pride in their way of going, and maybe why the Duncans weren't born to rule, the fridge stuffed that first night Gillian was to stay, and your old man that never had anything more than a coffee and a fag in the morning frying up the second she came down, your mum splashing the drinks and ardent about the politics, your dad eager to know about the law course, and you sat there then taking it as your due, for Gillian and for yourself, they were your parents and what else would they do, it took you till now to know.

The nights when you were a wee boy, sick and sorry for yourself with a cold or a sore throat, and your dad with his daud of butter rolled in sugar, just gulp it straight down Andy, it'll sort you right out, and actually it did seem to work, you still had no idea why, your mum ripping up an old sheet and mixing stuff up in a pot to slap a hot poultice on your chest, it felt warm and good for about five minutes and then just sticky and cold, and she said if you didn't like it then it must be doing you good, and never the slightest doubt in your mind that they loved you and cared about you and would do anything for you that they could. And actually it was a gift your mum had, to make everything fun, your Grandma talking to your Aunt Margaret when she thought you were asleep, you could stir that house Maggie, and she's sat in the middle of it happy as Larry playing with the weans, your mum smiling when you asked her about it, you have to remember your Grandma's from a different generation Andy, asking you if she sounded angry, and you said no she sounded pleased, and your mum really smiling then, she was pleased too, you and Louise crying with laughter when she would get you baking cakes or trying to make pancakes on Pancake Tuesday and one time you tried a gingerbread man, nothing ever turned out right, your mum trying to come up with uses for the ugly inedible things you produced, and then the three of you doing the dishes, the kitchen like a bomb site, and even that felt like some kind of hilarious game. Reading a story and your mum deciding you would make a wee play out of it for when your dad came in from work, a man with a spell put on him and for some reason a sausage stuck to the end of his nose, Louise was the sorcerer and you were the man, you cut out bits of paper to stick on the shade of the standard lamp for leaves, and a pair of tights rolled up for the sausage, and it wouldn't stick of course, you had to hold it on through the whole play, and your dad and all of you hooting through the whole thing, it was surely the single worst play ever produced.

The fascination you and Louise had with your mum's old typewriter, the keys so stiff it practically broke your fingers to type anything, and you had to keep winding the old knackered ribbon round to get any ink on the paper at all, but the hours you spent writing stories on it, and never once got further than one day Donald Duck or once upon a time Mickey Mouse before something went wrong, and the pages torn from school jotters scattered all over the house, just two or three words on all of them, one day Dobald or once upom a tine Mi or just ome dat, and you couldn't remember now if you even had a second line in your heads, you never needed it if you did, but still your mum said it was good, and it showed you both wanted to make some kind of mark on the world.

The day you went to Kilsyth with your dad on the bus, the rain pounding off the windows and you thought you would just be coming straight back, and when you got there the sun came out and you got chips and ice cream, your dad finding the dry river bed in the park and telling you it was places like this where gold was usually found, you looked diligently for ages and never bored for a second, you thought you were just unlucky not to find any, and when you got back your dad suggesting the two of you should draw a map so you could go back another time and carry on the search, him drawing and you colouring in, and carefully marking no gold here on the bits of it you'd searched already, and it was raining too the first time he took you with him to Littlehill, you weren't even going to go at first and then did for some reason, and your dad told you later he really thought you'd be fed up inside an hour, but you lasted the whole four hours no bother and never even thought about the miles you walked, and you hardly even cared about the golf part of it, just the beautiful rich green of it, and walking round there all grown up and talking a mile a minute to your dad. And before you went next time he cut down his old driver for you, and wound masking tape round the shaft for a grip, a beautiful neat job and no wonder he said, he was a winder to trade, and then you even got to play a wee bit once you were out of sight of the clubhouse, you were underage and supposed to be at least eight to get paid on properly, skelping away joyously, and counting your score dutifully like your dad told you, well into double figures by the time you got to the green, and then four or five putts, and your dad said that was pretty good, he'd like to see Jack Nicklaus do any better with just a driver. Haring off after your dad's ball when he had a good score going and hit a big slice over the hill, I fear for that one Andy, and all proud of yourself when you found it in the rough and brought it back to him, your dad calm and serious, how a golfer never lifted his ball and always played it where it lay, anything else was only cheating yourself, getting you to put it back exactly where you found it and even pushing it down a bit into the long grass though you told him it had been sitting right up, hacking his way out eventually and you could see he wanted to curse and swear but he just smiled grimly and said that was the great thing about the golf, it helped you to never get above yourself. Explaining to you too why he would never buy any balls from the wee boys that came up to you on the tees, it was well known they stole half of them, and why you had to go up and watch each other's shots at the blind holes, the guys that bought them were just encouraging it.

And then on your eighth birthday he wrote Passport to Littlehill on your card, and when you hit off the first tee for the first time ever all the guys standing around watching as usual, there was always a two hour wait to get on and any form of entertainment welcome, and you duffed it of course, the ball hardly rolling off the tee, and your dad smiling at first, aye you're a golfer now Andy, welcome to the club, and then seeing your stricken face, his hand on your shoulder, ach it's fine Andy, you'll get the next one, and you went down there and sconed it, the best you'd ever hit, a good distance and even up in the air for a wee bit, the guys round the tee still watching and you heard one of them say good shot wee man, and your dad came over and put an arm round you, and he said any idiot could hit a ball off a raised up tee, and it took real skill to hit one like that, and real guts too, and all of them watching you, he was really proud of you.

And then suddenly you were aware of Emmylou's voice in the brief, she was singing solo this time, and you knew all about it now, thc song she wrote after Gram's death from the drink and the drugs, and all his reckless energy and his dangerous talent needlessly, harmlessly gone, her beautiful voice aching from the loss of it, how she would walk half the length of America just to see his face again, and no avoiding the strangeness now, the feeling that time was short, and something was slipping away from you, and you thought still about Gillian's old man, and the strength in Gillian to make herself somehow into the person she was, and you knew you didn't have that same strength in you, but it seemed to you then that maybe you had a different kind at that, and you never felt more grateful that your mum and dad had made it so easy for you to be the person you were, or more glad that you were that person and not any of the ones you might have been, and it seemed to you too that you were ready to face it now, whatever it was that was coming.

12

The impulse to go and stand under the big clock, it was just for the hell of it, Gillian's train not due for a good half hour yet and hardly anyone around at this time in the morning, you could just sit down on one of the empty seats, but you were thinking of Holden waiting for old Sally Hayes, according to him no guy cared really about waiting, you just wanted your date to look terrific when she finally showed up, and not caring himself when Sally was late, only that she was a phony, and actually you always liked old Sally, maybe because she was so terrific-looking, but surely she had a lot to put up with from the bold boy, and still agreeing he could help her trim the tree at Christmas even after he called her a royal pain in the ass, she seemed quite kind really, but then you liked Cudahy the creepy old boozehound too, and him walking around the housc cxposing himself to poor Jane Gallagher, so maybe there wasn't a lot to be said for your judgment, or Nate's either for that matter, he was a big fan of the boozehound too, though he disagreed with you about old Sally, she was too shallow and materialistic for him. It was the nerves of course, you had no idea what was coming into your head next, but maybe it wasn't totally random at that because when they finally announced Gillian's train and you went up onto the platform and saw her, and then you saw the genuine delight in her face when she saw you, the feeling was just like Holden said, and the only thing in your mind was how completely terrific she looked, and how delighted you were to see her, and how much you loved her.

Straight round the corner for a coffee and she said she wasn't that tired really, she'd got a seat to herself on the train and a wee lie down for a good couple of hours, and the trouble coming into her eyes, the sweet diligent nature of her, you knew she wanted to get straight on with it and not keep you in the dark, and the strange calmness that came on you before she even said it, they wanted her down in London at least until after the Party Conference and probably beyond, and indefinitely really, that was the word she used and of course you knew it meant for good, the calmness in you deepening if anything, this was it and you were facing it, and you realized that you always knew what it would be, it was the people, they were coming for Gillian the same as they came for your Pop, and of course they wanted her, who wouldn't want her, you always knew they would want her, laughing and bantering with the folk at Faslane, and everyone loved her, young and old, all the badges gone in two seconds flat, and who else could they get in London that was like her, you might have had to ring them up and give them pelters yourself if they didn't want her.

And into your mind too that this was what you'd been waiting for, and working for, this was what had been always at stake, and you'd always known that too, and more than that even, that this was the day, this was the actual day, and both of you tired and drained, two hours of fitful sleep on a train for Gillian and you with hardly much more, and less actually, showered and dressed before five, there wasn't any point in just lying there any longer, and the caffeine would have to carry the two of you through it, that was just how it was, and when you said what about making today the day for Dunallan then, and you could leave talking about the rest of it till after that, Gillian smiling so gratefully, her eyes so instantly alive again, and she said that's a great idea Andy, and I really can't wait, I've been looking forward to it so much, and straight up to the counter for two more coffees, there was something near-mystical about it, the way she knew as surely as you did yourself that it was to be put right away from you now and left all for Dunallan, and how long had the sea been settling what would last and what would disappear, the trappings of the passing day put aside before antiquity and steadfast truth, the hollowness of outward things dismissed and only the things worthy of unconquerable life sanctified and revered, and the calmness spreading now to the furthest recesses of your heart, the image of it wholly alive in your mind, and it was the very quality and shape of right reason, and waiting for you, the anchor of your purest thoughts, the guide of your soul, unprofaned and universal and permanent, holding its silent eternal station.

And in the brief Gillian rattling away excitedly, not the slightest temptation to either of you to get into the issue of London and the rest, telling you what it was like in the flat she'd been staying at in Brighton, the preponderance of Oxbridge types, and if they weren't Oxbridge they were doing Peace Studies at Bradford, and hardly anyone from Scotland, or Wales for that matter, and she was the only one from Glasgow, lentil curries and cheap red wine and John Martyn's Solid Air and John Lennon's Imagine album, as if there had been nothing since, she played them the tape you made for her and the only thing they seemed to like at all was The Cure, but you defended John Lennon and Imagine, you'd only just bought it yourself, and that after hearing the two songs on Gillian's tape, and they were still the two you liked the best on the album, Crippled Inside, there was no hiding it if you were, and the wee jaunty tune perfect to disguise the bite of it, and then Oh My Love, Lennon's mind wide open for the first time in his life, his eyes able at last to see, and that was your favourite of all, and listened to nearly as much as Gram and Emmylou, getting to the coast in no time, and that with a stop at a call box to phone in sick, the early morning traffic light and fast, and mostly salesman types probably, trying to steal a march on the competition, and the waves clean and high, you knew they would be, the breeze perfectly offshore, and you dropped Gillian at the beach, she said she was happy to sit there and wait for you, the sun just starting to warm up the air and she was right that it was beautiful, you'd known that she would see that too, and driving the five minutes to Duke's garage to get your gear, you never felt calmer or more confident.

Changing into your wetsuit at Duke's instead of at the beach itself, and you knew fine well why, you wanted to walk straight down from the lay-by on the wee cliff and get onto the beach and into the water all in a oner, no delays and no hesitations, and when you hit the beach Gillian was sat hugging her knees, the big heavy jumper pulled down far over her jeans and she'd tied her hair back in bunches like a wee girl's, and when you shouted to her looking up and waving at you, her eyes eager and excited, achingly pretty, and she said you looked good yourself in your gear, and a million questions about your board, and the kind of waves there were today and was it good that they were breaking to both sides like that, and she asked you where she should stand, you said the wee cliff might give the best view, but she said she wanted to be closer than that, and as close as possible, and you were secretly glad, wanting her close yourself, and in the end she took her shoes and socks off and rolled up the bottom few inches of her jeans, gasping at the cold of it when the white water surged over her toes, and grabbing your shoulder to help steady herself, the two of you hooting, and when you reached the lineup and sat straddling your board, sucking down air and waiting for your breath to come back, you never paddled so single-mindedly before, you saw her in motion, the wee graceful dance steps back and forth in the baby surf, trying to feel the surge and drag of it around her feet without looking down, her eyes fixed totally on you, and her whole face alive with anticipation as soon as she saw you looking at her, she waved at you and shouted something, you couldn't catch what it was but only your name at the end of it, and you waved back and then looked behind you at the set coming in, you let the first two or three waves go by, and then you saw your wave, you flattened yourself on the board and paddled hard, the movements easy and practised and natural and right, and you knew in your quiet soul that this was who you were and this was what you did, your trust never more firm or resolute either in what you might become.

And the sea in fact seeming almost playful on this long appointed day, in lightsome mood, this first wave sweet and gracious and indulgent, you took off at the last possible moment, but your commitment to catching it never in doubt, the wave knew it, waiting for you almost, and you took the drop at the highest part, nose pointed straight down the face, accepting the magnanimous gift of it in every part of you, every movement of your hands and arms and legs and feet, giving all you had yourself of power and speed, and racing into the bottom turn, still you tried to ease round as gracefully as you could, to respect the mood of the wave, its indulgence and its generosity, and Gillian herself so graceful you knew on the shore, but still the cut was deep and decisive, the water spraying extravagantly as the inside rail carved its line, and you were frontside now along the smooth glassy wall of it, and all at once the impulse to connect yourself more intimately yet, and you reached out and touched it with your hand, you felt the tiny shift it made in your line, and instantly your angle was one you'd never taken on any face before, and never could have imagined even, you felt the wave endorse it and applaud it, the exuberant white spray at your hand now as well as your feet, the joyous lines you were drawing visible a moment on the face and then gone forever, and of course that was just how it should be.

And it came to you then that your wave that very first day had been no fluke after all, the bond given and the vows made before you even knew it, and yet you'd honoured the debt you incurred unknowingly on that day, and ready now to honour what was being extended to you this day if it took you the rest of your life, and your heart beat higher than ever to be vouchsafed such a privilege, the joy of it was everywhere you looked, in the roil and bubble of the white water behind you, the icy sharp cold of the wave on your hand, the breathless wilderness of clouds above, and when you glanced round to the shore you saw Gillian running, the effort to keep up with you as you angled along the wall, her whole face pink already from the exertion, the water splashing high round her ankles, and her jeans would be soaked, her big jumper discarded somehow and lying crumpled on the sand, and her tee-shirt underneath was bright green with thick yellow writing on it, you knew it would be Friends of the Earth or Greenpeace or the like, and the whole tumult and dance of it in your mind, it seemed to you that you never saw such an impassioned sight of colours and forms in your life before.

Kicking out and over the top of the wave as it started to close out, you felt almost ungrateful to take your leave of it like that, you could have stayed with it easily all the way to Gillian and the beach, but the feeling so strong in your heart that it was out here and nowhere else that all was to be settled, paddling strongly back to the lineup, and you saw Gillian follow your progress, walking now, but still waving her arms excitedly and clapping too and cheering, you caught your name again on the breeze, and on the next wave a new privilege extended, your bottom turn too bold and you climbed high up the face, you saw the lip rear up towards you, and just as quickly the instinct came, and your weight went hard to your back foot, your front foot guiding the board round, arms balancing you, and you were already well into the turn when your board hit the lip, cornering and driving hard and you made the turn off the top, you'd never even contemplated such a thing, and yet already it was done, the debt incurred and the passion to honour it rising up in you, and this time a gentler bottom turn, into trim along the face, and your hand on the wave again, you let it tell you when the time was right, and then cutting back once and then twice to the pocket, the gift of fresh speed and energy from the most critical part of the wave, and the turns themselves smooth and deeply set, your board bounding high off the oncoming white water and back into trim, and then your hand back on the wave, a new angle and a new line, and it was all you could do to make yourself kick out this time, you could hear Gillian hooting and cheering on the beach, and the sound seeming like it was carried to you from all directions at once.

And then wave after wave, right-breaks and left-breaks, frontside and backside, the lineup the same for both on this day, and that another debt you would honour, the waves themselves telling you which to choose each time, clean powerful turns and smooth arcing cutbacks, and your hand always now on the cold rushing face, the infinite potential for fresh new lines on every wave, and late in the session even coming off the lip on the backside, you looked over your shoulder to see the break of it, and trying somehow to judge the turn, so far by rights beyond your ability, but you pushed down hard with your back foot, and your weight onto the inside rail, your board climbing back up the face, and at the lip over full to the opposite rail, leveraging with bent arms, and hard again on your back foot at the tail, and miraculously it was done, plunging straight down the face now and into the trough, the flash of green and yellow and Gillian's flushed excited face at the very edge of your vision, or maybe just in your mind, you felt the strong breeze in your face, the sluice and spray of the turn, and then so fast along the face, in the pocket and just ahead of the curl, your back to the wave and your eyes on the shore, and no doubt about it this time, Gillian running with you along the water's edge, the flashes still of green and yellow, and the explosion of white round her ankles, another dance of images, and still you were leaving her further and further behind, and you knew suddenly then that this was to be your last wave of the day, the craving to be with Gillian at last, to be assured that it was all as visible and real for her as it was for you, that London and the rest of it was nothing after all but a nagging dream of vain and pointless struggle, and that here at Dunallan was simple reality and self-presented truth, a genuine republic where distinction lay open to all that came, where the proud workings of the soul were properly valued and sanctioned and recompensed, where the air was free to breathe and there was nothing for the heart to dread.

Then into the channel and paddling for the beach, you saw Gillian step back onto the drier sand, but still watching you, and waiting for you, eager and excited, and when you came out her arms straight round your neck, and she was hugging you and kissing you, not giving a fuck that you were getting her tee-shirt nearly as wet as her jeans, they were soaked already to the knees and above, laughing at how salty you were, and her own clothes would be salt-marked too, and she said that was fantastic Andy, the most amazing thing she ever saw, she'd give anything to be able to do it herself, she was dying to learn, and ready to get in there and start this very moment if she'd had any gear, you would have to teach her, not that she'd ever be half as good as you were, you obviously had a total gift for it, and that was hardly a surprise to her she said, she'd known you must have from the first moment you told her about your fly wee jaunts outside the Vale, the look you had in your eyes, and the same look you'd had half the night actually, she'd been dying to know what put it there, and so honoured when Mack brought you out and you chose her to confide in.

Rattling away breathlessly while you stood there on the beach and listened, you'd never even known that about the night you met her in the Vale, and you weren't even shivering in the strong cool breeze, though normally by now you'd have been up at the brief already and into your changing routine, you felt the warmth spread from somewhere deep inside you, smiling and laughing with Gillian, she never looked so wonderful, and managing to get in with the odd great and right and thanks, and whether it was caffeine or adrenaline or both she was still going a million words a second, and all you could do was listen and nod in the right places, the warmth and the happiness of it, Gillian on again about the amazing gift you had, and weren't you dying to share it, and the sudden feeling like you'd jumped off the wee cliff, your guts left behind and falling and falling, as if something inside you knew where it was going the second she started, how incredible it was to think that there were kids in Easterhouse just an hour's drive from all this, and the ones in Craigmillar even closer for that matter, it was right in their back yard, and imagine the difference it could make to their lives, to experience something like this, she'd give anything to have something so fantastic to share, the gift that you had, and the opportunity.

And all you could think was that she'd brought the people right with her, right here to this place of all places, and Gillian of all people, they'd cut your throat for ten shillings, cut you and beat you and leave you to bleed, and you saw them stood where Gillian was standing now, on the very ground where you'd tried to save her, their sullen insolent wee coupons, bored and resentful, surfing just another tedious gym class for them, the sea another grim youth club hall, staring you down, daring you to try and reach them, and you felt the sudden terrible silence, you thought it was only in your head, and a few moments more even till you saw that it was real, that Gillian had stopped for a breather, and she was looking at you and waiting, her eyes still ardent from the excitement of it, the Easterhouse kids and the Craigmillar kids and all you would do for them, waiting for you to speak, and to match her zeal with your own, and you managed to mumble that you weren't sure you took her meaning, you knew you should say more, but all your fine thoughts and fine words suddenly gone, you said the only ones that came to you, it's a test of a surfer to ride alone, you shouldn't have to rely on anyone but yourself.

Gillian's eyes puzzled just a moment, and then looking at you sheepishly, and you saw there was more on her mind than whatever it was you meant, you hardly knew yourself what that was anyway, and how she should just come out and say it, she'd meant to let you get changed and warmed up first, you must be freezing and exhausted both, but fuck it, she'd started now, and you must know anyway that she wasn't really talking about Easterhouse or Craigmillar, she'd been asking the London ones down in Brighton, and there was a scheme going that could have been tailor-made for you, it was all football and boxing and athletics for now, but no reason why it shouldn't be surfing too, and she even knew some of the people herself, good people, you would like them, strapped for cash now but that would change, the Left were organizing to get control of the GLC, and she said you should see those kids down there Andy, not just the unemployment and the crime and the poverty but the racism, the hatred and the poison of it, you wouldn't believe their lives. The ardour in her eyes again, if they could experience just a fraction of what you'd shown her today, what it would bring to them, the hope and the joy of it, and she'd phoned the British Surfing Federation, there were waves you could surf at Newquay and in Devon, and even some place in East Anglia, they were all drivable from London, a minibus or whatever, and anyway even if all you did was just go round talking to them, the passion you had for it, just that alone could make such a difference, you could change their lives forever.

And into your head your own letter from the Federation, welcome to the world of surfing Andy, your life will never be the same, the thrill it gave you, and the thought inside you somewhere that this was everything you'd hoped for surely, Gillian restored to you, the long dread of losing her gone, and who gave a fuck if it was London or where it was, all the trouble she'd gone to, and how thrilled she was herself to have Dunallan vindicate her own highest hopes, the least you should do was talk about it you knew. And yet falling and falling, the shock of it like pain, and the last thing you could do in this place was just go along, you heard the despair in your voice sounding like anger, and you knew you should stop, but you couldn't stop, the sullen insolent faces of them, and you suddenly knew that they were right to be sullen, and right to be insolent, how many times had you sat there feeling the same way yourself, the smug pompous lectures from the ones that always knew what was best for you, and what was best for everyone, and you heard yourself, who were you to tell kids in London they should learn to surf, who were you to tell them anything, and who was anyone to tell anyone anything, it was that exactly that was the problem, everyone telling everyone elsc what to do, and never the space to just find out what you were meant to do, and surfing the furthest thing there could ever be from such oppressive capers, you didn't find surfing, it had to find you, and all you could hope was to be left alone to let it, fuck anyone who tried to interfere, and fuck anyone who tried to make anyone else do anything.

The pallor suddenly in Gillian's face, the tiredness all at once in her eyes, and you'd have given anything to take back what you said, the sweet kind nature of her, and fuck all the chance she would ever make anyone do anything they didn't want to do, you tried to tell her so but you couldn't, the tears in your own eyes as you saw them coming to hers, and she spoke so quietly and so softly, her voice breaking with the pain of it, and she said she knew you were right, and always knew it probably, she just hoped so much it could be different, but of course it couldn't, she saw it now, and it was what she loved you for, all the community you needed in the waves, and maybe in the team, but she was different, she knew that too, she had to share whatever she knew, and give whatever she had, and forcing a smile, it broke your heart, she had to admit it, she wanted to change the world, and she needed to go to London just as much as you needed to stay here at Dunallan, the tears in her eyes and the cold breeze on her wet salty clothes, and the two of you stood now shivering, the waves breaking ever further away as the tide went out.

13

The QM bar pretty much what you expected, big Graham true to his word, and no problem at all in finding someone to sign you both in, you sailed past the old guy at the door, and then the groups of students lounging around the low tables, some of them had been there all day by the looks of them, their canvas satchels and the odd scuffed-looking sports bag propped carelessly against the legs of chairs, the books and notes poking out of them, piles of empty glasses and debris on every table, and the brightest source of light in the whole place was the puggie going its dinger at the far wall. Graham taking a moment to get his eyes used to the gloom, then spotting some of his team over in a corner, and the two of you went over, you recognized the guys that sang oh my Stalin and the Berlin Wall song your very first time at the flat, and this the first time you'd seen them since in fact, the stab of pain from it, and they obviously knew about you and Gillian, they pushed their lips tight together and raised their chins up and nodded sympathetically when they saw you.

The loss of hope, and things to hope for, Graham surprising you when you said it before at the flat, though you probably should have known, the books piled everywhere in his room, he was very well read for all they kicked him out the Uni, you'd assumed it was mostly all politics and philosophy but no, he said that was Wordsworth wasn't it, and it took you a second even to realise that it was, you said aye do you like him, and Graham, he's okay, a bit reactionary for myself, and then Shelley now, there was a poet, you let him rattle on, sipping at your tumbler of the Buckie, the strong sweet taste of it, grateful for the chance to nod and smile, your mind relentless, turning it over and over, the loss of hope, and things to hope for, and why had you pestered him to see it, the room more or less as it always had been, even the guitar still there, and Gillian always adamant she was just learning and only knew the two chords, and laughing, refusing to play anything for you, she couldn't sing a note either she said, the riddie she had when you would keep on about it, you never loved her more, but all her clothes gone, you saw the pity and embarrassment in Graham's eyes when you opened the big wardrobe and couple of drawers, the bed stripped bare, and when you reached out and laid a hand down on the mattress Graham with his hand on your shoulder, and leading you gently away, I told you it was a bad idea big man, and then fuck this, come on we'll tan the rest of the Buckie and away down the QM, you can crash in my room the night, smiling myopically at you, his eyes half-cut and kind, he was letting you buy he said.

The feeling of unreality as you peeled off your wetsuit in Duke's garage, a desultory rub with the towel and pulling your clothes on, wetsuit and towel into a bin-bag and flung into the boot of the brief, you'd be ashamed to let Duke and the others see your gear in such a state. Picking up Gillian and then parked at the first place you saw, the quaint wee tea shop so incongruous a setting that you even managed a smile at it, and Gillian making it odder still, you both needed the calories she said, the waitress arriving with the pot of tea for two on the tray, unloading the cups and saucers, scones and cakes and butter and jam, side plates and cutlery and fuck knew what all, Gillian still with her wet jeans but her tee-shirt nearly dry from the heat in the brief, the tide-marks of salt forming from where she'd hugged you, it seemed to belong to another time already, and you felt salty and itchy and clatty yourself, your hair matted and spiked, forcing mouthfuls of scone and cake down your throat with gulps of tea, you couldn't taste a thing anyway, trying to hold back the tears and apologizing over and over, you'd have said anything not to lose her.

But Gillian strong now, and calm, it wasn't about what you'd said, true though it was, and jolting her out of her pipedreams she had to admit, it was about what she'd seen, and what you'd both felt, you knew as well as she did that you'd only said what you'd have both come to realise sooner or later, and when you said no you hadn't, your head was full of mince, and everything you'd said was gibbers, you didn't give a fuck about any of it, only about her, and not losing her, she just smiled sadly at you, that might be true right now, and for a month or two even, but there was a bigger picture, you both knew it fine well, and why would you do it to yourselves, looking at you so lovingly, the only thing was to end it now, and why keep torturing yourselves with more talk. But you couldn't help it, talking and talking on the drive back to Glasgow, apologizing and pleading, arguing and reasoning, how much you loved her and needed her and couldn't be without her, Gillian more and more tired and pale, she cried the whole way back to her flat, and all the time you knew her decision was made, and no more chance of changing it than of catching a wave after it was past you or turning back the tide.

The groans from Graham's team as he produced the crumpled bit of card from his back pocket and started unfolding it, he had four stamps already and needing another eight for the special free glass, and it seemed you were all on Guinness the rest of the night to get him his glass and the couple more he needed for the set, the promotion had only another night to go he said. And your first time drinking the stuff in fact, the taste different, strong and thick, but actually easier to get down than lager once you got used to it, the others leaving you to your conversation, and only interrupted when a round fell due, the groans and hilarity as Graham went to his pocket for his card, and an extra loud dose of it when you got up for his round as well as your own, he treated them to a chorus of owe us a living, and you joined in for the hell of it, course they do, course they do, they owe us a living, course they fucking do.

Graham wiping the foam from the Guinness off the bits of beard round his top lip, listening intently and nodding, and you told him you hadn't been able to face going out with the team in the weeks since it happened, you'd managed a few pints with Allie the couple of nights he'd called round for you, and you knew he'd put the word out from there, they'd all steered clear for the duration and no chance of any of them being that tactful without a heads-up, and you told Graham what Allie said when you asked would it be okay to wade up to the Steeple instead of the Vale for a wee bit, have they got bevvy there Andy, and when you laughed and said you thought so he said sounds minted to me then, and what the fuck are we waiting for, and Graham laughing himself, good guy, good guy. And Allie was a good guy, rattling away about motors and the new bands he was into and the latest team capers while you sat there blank and numb, he pretended not to notice or maybe really didn't notice, and either way not judging or offering advice, just as content to sit in silence with you too, savouring the taste of his pint, and he said it was good to get Fosters for a change, you should maybe get a petition up to get it put in at the Vale, it tasted sweet almost. The bev actually helping you get off to sleep on those nights, but still your eyes coming open again as always, half-dreaming, the shapes in the dark room almost persuading you somehow that Gillian was there, you learned not to question it, and not to think yourself into coming fully awake, and able that way to get back over for a few hours till it was time to get up for work.

But you knew what the rest of them would say, Mack and Joe and Waldo, for fuck's sake big man it's just a bit of fanny, you need to hold your head high, and to hell with her, she's had her chance, and Nate no doubt with his own sarcastic take, and maybe you were wrong about all of them but you just couldn't have stood it if you were right, you didn't give a fuck about holding your head high or any of the rest of it, and ready to whine and plead and crawl as low as anyone might ask if there was any chance it would bring Gillian back, you only wished it could be that easy. Big Graham just about nodding his head off at that, fucking right big man, fucking right, it's all bullshit, and how he'd gone to Amsterdam a couple of summers back, he had some pals squatting in a krak there, and nicer actually than Bellingham Terrace by the way, running water and electricity and everything, but the guy that ran the black work on the docks taking a scunner to the lot of them, they hadn't two guilders to rub together and nothing else for it if they wanted to eat, down the street market every day at closing time, hoovering up all the old veggies and fruit that had got dropped on the ground, and all the folk looking at you, you cared at first and after five minutes you didn't give a fuck, the blank stare you gave them, it was them that looked away.

And maybe it was the Guinness, you knew you were well away with it by now, and the whole team around you pretty much honkus plonkus too, Graham with three cards filled and his free glasses clinking away in his long coat when you finally staggered up the road to the flat, but it seemed to you then that he understood what you were talking about better than anyone, and you listened when he leaned in close to you, it was all bullshit, you should feel just however you felt and not give a fuck, and anyone that said different send the fuckers to him, the two of you with your arms round each other's shoulders weaving your way back to Bellingham Terrace, giving it laldy with the no nay nevers, and you were going for death Graham said, the bottle of Buckie produced from somewhere and tanned between you for a nightcap, crashing out finally on the floor of his room, the man himself snoring away happily on the bed, and you were still up in time for work in the morning, you knew you would be, always wide awake at five sharp nowadays, it would take more than alcoholic poisoning to stop you, leaving a wee note for Graham, thanks for everything, and you said you'd be in touch, you didn't really think you would be, only a matter of time before Gillian picked up the rest of her stuff, and then not even the pain to go back for.

Glad in fact that your work was there, the discipline of it holding you together somehow as everything else came apart, you volunteered for every extra shift going, and your Manager even onto you when he saw how heavy you were loading the bag in the mornings, for fuck's sake Andy, leave something for the rest of them, but still too much time always to fill, and most of it the time you'd used for surfing truth be told, you hadn't been back to Dunallan since that day, not the faintest notion for it, and in all honesty you'd be pushed to say if you would ever surf again. It was ridiculous, you knew it fine well, as much logic in blaming Dunallan and surfing for the loss of Gillian as there was in thinking the white-haired old dears and painted-up kids at Faslane could turn into a rampaging mob, but anyway it was how you felt, you just couldn't help it, and surely big

Graham was right about that, you felt how you felt, and not the slightest inclination to go back to Dunallan after what it did to you, it was wrong and stupid maybe to feel like that but still it was how it was, and taking you all your time even to finally clean off and dry down your wetsuit and put it away in the back of your big bedroom cupboard, you damn near ruined the thing.

Gillian's tape still playing exclusively in the brief, you knew that wasn't a good idea either, but as much chance of changing it as there was of driving off to the coast and skipping merrily into the sea with your board, and worse than that even, pushing the eject button on the stereo when you got home from work and taking the tape up to play in your bedroom hour after hour, hardly an interest in any of your own records, the ones you'd always thought would be how you'd feel, magnanimous and rueful and mature, they didn't speak to you at all, and the only one you played over and over was Wreckless Eric of all people, his cover of Crying, Waiting, Hoping, and something about the theatrical, histrionic way he sang it that was true and right and genuine to you for some reason. But always inexorably back to Gillian's tape, constantly rewinding for Gram and Emmylou, Love Hurts, the aching harmony of their voices, and the sadness of it soaking through into every part of you now, life's mysterious weight of pain and fear. And then Boulder to Birmingham, Emmylou's beautiful heartbroken voice, the hardest part was knowing you'd survive, and that was exactly right, your dad taking you for a pint at the Steeple, trying to cheer you up, and no idea what the fuck to do when you just suddenly lost it and sat there in quiet floods of tears, the crowded bustling pub and the wee undertone of panic coming into his voice, how Gillian was a bonnie lassie all right, and he'd been very fond of her himself as you knew, and your mum too, but you were just young, you'd be over it way sooner than you'd believe, and meet another nice lassie in no time, and you tried your best to pull it together and not embarrass him any more, wanting to tell him that you knew all that, but just that it was the hardest part, the decision to survive, and to let go of the pain, and let go of Gillian, the thought of surviving without her was what was unbearable, the loss of hope, and things to hope for, life's mysterious weight of pain and fear, and the tears still rolling down your face, you managed to get out that you were sorry, you were sure you'd be all right in a minute.

Then the day it happened, not that you suddenly let her go, or even felt remotely better, you felt worse if that was possible, but just that something changed, and you knew it was the start of it, getting over it or surviving it or whatever you wanted to call it, on the phone to her in London, and that was familiar enough, not to your credit, you'd tried everything to leave her be, and not to call, but you just couldn't seem to control yourself, and starting her very first day in the job, surely nothing wrong in just checking she'd got down there okay, secretly hoping to hear that she hadn't made it, her old man had stopped her somehow, forced her to stay in Glasgow and finish her law degree, and how would that be for an unholy alliance, you and her old man in cahoots, both trying to hold onto her for your different selfish reasons. But you knew anyway that she wouldn't see her old man in her road, or the law either, the only point of it ever was to maybe help her get into politics, and now she was in, what would she need the law for, and when she came on the phone you said was the journey okay, and was the place she was staying in all right, and how was work, you could hear all the activity and excitement and camaraderie in the background, the stab of pain it gave you, and still there long after you hung up the phone, and resolving that whatever else you did you'd never put yourself through that again.

And a couple of days later you called again, some bullshit excuse, and convincing yourself it was a good and genuine reason to be in touch, and then the same pattern time after time, the Oxbridge voices that answered, friendly enough the first couple of times, then cold and then straight-out hostile, you could hear the tightness of them, the barely suppressed anger when they told you to hold on, and you knew they were begging Gillian to let them tell you to fuck off out of it and leave her alone, both of you close to tears always by the end of it, and she would say that she had to get back, there was so much to do, and the conference so close, but still always taking the phone, never letting them make an excuse for her, and you knew she would defend you to them, the sweet loyal nature of her, not that you gave a fuck about them, they could think whatever they wanted, and fuck them if they thought they knew a millionth as much as you did about the person she was.

Watching bits of the conference on the telly between shifts and on the news at night, and Gillian phoning you on the Friday just as she promised she would, she said she was in the lobby of the Imperial Hotel, and you could hear it all going on behind her, the buzz and the celebrations, and she could hardly hear you she said, they were all going for a few drinks but she didn't think she would last long, she was totally knackered. And you said she sounded it, and congratulations, you'd been following it all, and rhyming it all off, you had it carefully memorized, mandatory reselection carried and an electoral college to elect the leader, unilateral disarmament and out of the Common Market passed overwhelmingly, and the one on the punters writing the manifesto just narrowly beaten, you said don't worry, you'll get that one next year, standing ovations for Tony Benn and all the other left-wingers, she must be very proud of herself, and she started to say well it was a team effort really, and everyone pitching in, and then stopped, the wee laugh, you loved to hear it and it broke your heart too, and she said fuck it, and yes, she was really proud of herself, and that this was just the start of it, we're really going to do it this time Andy.

Then forcing yourself to let the days pass, you held out as long as you could, and finally made the call, the usual tight-arsed Oxbridge tones telling you to hold on, and then Gillian at last, she sounded so light and happy that you fell into it with her, you could tell she was still on a high from the conference, and she admitted yes she was, an open secret that Callaghan's speech at Blackpool was his farewell as leader, and the wheels in motion to get Tony Benn in, they were working flat out on it she said, the CLPs heavily in favour but so much work to do on the MPs and the leadership of the unions, they were always a mile behind the grassroots, and you listened contentedly, you were interested actually, and even chipping in, clued up from big Graham and your mum and the stuff you'd watched on the telly, and you and Gillian chatting away like old pals, light and friendly, she was laughing and joking with you again, and you willed yourself not to jinx it, so happy when she said I really do have to get back to it Andy and everything was still just as easy and light as ever, you said okay, you'd talk to her again soon, and she said right, and that'll be great Andy, and bye for now then.

And it was a good while after you put down the phone that you finally registered the relief you'd heard in her voice when she said those last words, and registered too what it meant, the relief that maybe you could talk away together like old pals now, all the rest of it put behind you and over, and in your head Emmylou's beautiful heartbroken voice, and it was never truer, the hardest part was knowing you'd survive, and accepting in some way what you'd lost, facing the simple truth that it was gone, and the tears back in your eyes now as you braced yourself to try.

14

The sound of Mack's voice on the phone, you could hardly believe how much it cheered you, the last weeks just a black hole, and the less said the better, and Mack, it's a team wade to the Glencairn big man, full turn-out required on pain of expulsion, and how your membership was already getting looked into, you and Allie both, he knew all about your wee cosy jaunts up to the Steeple together, the gayfruits that you were, your coats on a shoogly peg, and how he'd told Allie the same thing, the Committee were taking a very dim view, and on and on, you could tell he had a big spiel prepared, all ready to have to talk you round, and determined to do it, you loved him for that, but still you took some wicked pleasure in cutting in, and you said Friday night then, fucking minted, you were definitely up for it, and Mack at a loss for words for a second or two at the other end of the line, surely a first, you felt quite proud of yourself actually.

The honk of the horn and running out to the Mark III, you felt a faint echo of Joe pulling the wheelies in the school car park, the uncomplicated thrill of it then, and the stab of nostalgia for something so recent, you had to smile at it yourself. Off up to the Glencairn, Joe driving like a maniac, you and Allie and Mack lurching about in the back, the echo bouncing its way to the Hughie Machine at the Kelvin Hall, and you told them at the time you weren't supposed to have three of you on it, the bar daudie not even properly locked in, and you in the middle then the same as now, a miracle you weren't pitched right out of the thing, they thought it was hilarious and you screaming your head off the whole time, the bastards never let you forget it to this day.

And Joe with Graham Parker on the stereo, you smiled at that too, the subject matter not exactly on point but the title surely was, You Can't Be Too Strong, and something so right too about the self-consciously fake bravado of it, refusing to cry, and deciding to rejoice with your mates instead, you gave it a big yeeee-haaaa for the hell of it, and Joe joining right in with you, it was him that started it months back, some lassie telling him he put her in mind of Bo Duke, a dark-haired version she said, and she was the one that went weak at the knees when he gave her a flex of the neck muscles according to Joe, though Nate disagreed, it was her eyes were weak according to him, and her head obviously. But still the Mark III becoming The General for a while after that until Joe took a scunner to the Dukes for some reason, and now into his Mad Max capers, he loved the targets Mel Gibson had on his windscreen, and making his own version with wee strips of masking tape on the sunspecs, not even Joe was mental enough to stick targets on his actual windscreen, the cops already with enough of an eye out for the Mark III as it was, but anyway the ones on the shades giving pretty much the same effect so he claimed, and Nate now in the front seat for his big lanky legs, hooting and calling out for them, get the targets on Joe, come on give us the targets, he thought they were the greatest things ever.

The lounge of the Glencairn stowed as always on a Friday but your luck was in seemingly, a big team leaving just as you arrived, guys and lassies both, and the place always popular with the couples for some reason, Sultans of Swing never off the jukebox, you thought of the Glencairn straight off now whenever you heard it, and Joe Jackson blasting away when you walked in, It's Different for Girls, and that was another one actually, even the B-side getting regular laldy, you would see people's lips moving at the chorus, she don't care no more, she gets paid on Friday. Shuffling your way round into the big semi-circular booth at the far wall, Nate away up to the bar, and the lassie coming over for the empty glasses from the previous team, giving it the big sigh as she looked at you, and maybe she remembered you and Mack from when you were in a few months back, the big silver boat of tartare sauce she put down on the table and when she came back for it you'd tanned the whole thing, it was supposed to be for everybody she said, and all the families in for their bar lunches, not even a bit amused when you both cracked up, and refusing to believe you that you really didn't know, but then maybe she just wasn't over-happy in her work at the best of times, you could hardly blame her for that. Cracking up now too when Joe came back from sorting out the jukebox and sat down, the air of quiet satisfaction, and then Sultans of Swing coming on, what else, all of you giving it fuck's sake Joe, winding him up, you knew fine well the thing took a million years to play anybody's selections, and still folk chucking their money into it like they never heard music before, but Joe anyway with the indignant riddie, I never put that shite on, and how he'd put on Dexy's and Althea and Donna and The Jam, and the rest of you, yeah yeah, whatever you say Joe, you could tell he had half an ear the whole rest of the night whenever the song changed, Going Underground at least doing the business for him a good few times, but fuck all the sign of the other two ever, and just as well Nate said, that Althea and Donna thing was gowping, and had poor Mrs

Bannigan not been embarrassed enough already in her life.

Hard to tell if things really were a bit awkward at first, and the team avoiding the subject of Gillian, or if it was all in your head, and you knew there was a fair chance of that, you weren't daft, no reason for everyone else to be obsessed with it just because you were, and not for the first time you thanked fuck for Waldo, off his shift at the station and straight over on his ridiculous wee 50cc Honda, bouncing in like Evel Knievel in the leather gear, jacket and breeks both, and carrying the full-face helmet with the glass visor and everything, even the table of bikey-wikey boys nodded respectfully at him, it was obvious they took him for one of their own, and probably thinking he had a big muckle Suzuki or something parked outside. And Waldo announcing now he'd been up to eighty-five coming over the Campsies, and when Joe said how the fuck was that possible, there was more power in a lassie's hair dryer than the thing he had, he said it was no bother, you just had to get across the tank. Then seeing you, and you were the very man he'd been looking for apparently, sorry to hear about you and the lassie Gillian, she was a total ride, and by the way could he sniff the passenger seat in your brief, he'd been meaning to ask you for yonks and no time to lose now, he was only hoping he hadn't left it too long. And it seemed to you that it wasn't just your imagination, the tension really broken, and you hooted as much as the rest of them, you wondered if Waldo knew how much of a genius he was, and you were sure he had some idea from the wee look he gave you, a fake Gillian set up just like that, the lassie that was a total ride, and that you could laugh and joke about, anyone could say anything, and the real Gillian free and off on her own hundreds of miles away, unaffected by any of it, and anyway just an old pal these days, you could phone her if you wanted, though you doubted now you ever would.

Mack coming through to the bar with you to help you carry your round back, the conspiratorial tone, how he'd bumped into Karen Clarke down the street, you said really, and he said aye, did you not always have a wee thing for her, you wondered what the punch-line was going to be, but Mack totally sincere as far as you could tell, how she'd deefied her man and broken off the engagement, and she was asking for you, he'd told her you would give her a call, and how she was definitely up for it, you knew you could trust your Uncle Bobby, and howking a wee grubby slip of paper out of the pocket of his jeans, he'd even looked up her old dears' number for you in the book, you took it and said thanks, you'd think about it.

Then Mack with the three pint jars gripped no bother in his big mitts, leaving you to pay for the round and bring the rest, the thought occurring to you and you said could you just keep it to yourselves by the way, the Karen Clarke thing, you weren't even sure you were going to do anything about it, and what were they like through there about stuff like that, and Mack, of course big man of course, and how you could rely on your Uncle Bobby, he knew fine what the score was with you and no problem at all, don't even give it another thought, and in the half minute it took you to settle up and come through with the other three pints you saw that the fucker had the whole team told, Waldo slapping you on the back, he said the Clarke lassie definitely liked her Nat King, it was well known, and if you had a good dick you were in there by the way. And if that wasn't enough, Joe leering at you too, you were a horny big wanker he said, and straight over to put your names up for doubles at the pool, he put you up on the board as HBW, and when your turn finally came up the guys at the table shouting HBW, HBW, and Joe, all pleased with himself, his arm stretched right over your napper and pointing down at you, aye HBW, this is him here, this is the HBW here, the rest of them hooting at the big riddie you had, and what else could you do, you shrugged and had a wee hoot yourself.

But still it served the fucker right really, quite proud of his skills at the pool and your arses felt the very first game, you and him teamed up against the guys that were on the table, and you saw right away why they'd been on it the whole night practically, Joe with the big macho break skiting the balls everywhere, but nothing went down, and that was it, you never even got a shot after that, their first guy all the way to the black in about two seconds, and then potting that as well, tapping the pocket nonchalantly with the tip of his cue to let you know where it was going, and just like that you were grannied, the guy swaggering round the table and smiling over at his bird, you could see she was quite impressed with him, and Joe pointing over at the guy, still poncing around and preening himself, the big stage whisper to you, there's only one thing to do when you're in a state like that Andy, sit down and have a pull at your plonker, you nearly choked on your pint trying not to laugh, and the guy and his mate heard it of course, drawing daggers at Joe, he just looked calmly back at them, you knew he wouldn't see guys like that in his road, and sure enough they looked away sharp enough when they got the proper measure of him, the big show of chalking their cues and trying to decipher the next set of initials on the board, and you and Joe sauntering back to join the team, you could tell Joe felt better about the grannying now, and you did yourself actually if you were honest.

Then just at last orders, and all of you half-cut or worse, Mack with the passing mention of your fly wee jaunts and you thought fuck it, in for a penny in for a pound, and you told them quickly about Dunallan and surfing, you said you'd been quite into it there for a wee while but kind of scunnered with it now if you were honest, and Nate, another of the famous Duncan enthusiasms then, it kind of cheered you in a way, you hadn't known you were famous for anything, but anyway only too happy to agree, the neatness of it pleasing you too, a fake Dunallan and fake surfing to go with the fake Gillian, and even less danger with them than with Gillian of betraying all they'd meant to you with self-serving talk, team interest in the whole thing all but gone already, it was obvious the mystery of it had been more intriguing than the fact. And fair play to them, Mack and Allie doing their best to show willing, a question or two about how surfing worked, and was it like yon picture you'd watched the time the porn was off at the Classic Grand, and Joe, you must have been knackered from all the driving, the M8 was a fucker in his considered opinion, but it was clear they were only too happy to get back to previous topics as soon as possible, relieved when they saw you had no appetite for it either, and then all of you hooting again in no time at some story of Waldo's, you felt another wave of relief to get that one over so smoothly as well.

Joe refusing to let Waldo anywhere near his wee bike in the state he was in, surprisingly responsible about things like that, and always sticking scrupulously to his couple of shandics when he had the brief, but as mental as always of course the second he got behind the wheel, the four of you poured into the back now, and Nate still riding shotgun, deigning to allow Waldo's big ridiculous helmet on the floor at his feet, and thank fuck for that, there was fuck all the room for it in the back with you. The tape straight into the stereo, an Allie special, the whole brief shaking from the noise of it, the bass turned up full and you were all giving it maximum laldy on the choruses, Saturday's Kids and Protex Blue and Hanging Around, and then on Babylon's Burning Joe giving it Porter's house is burning, and all of you cracking up, and Waldo shouting you could go down there the now, he had some fireworks in the garage, just tie them onto a tree and then light light light, five of you instantly up for it and Nate twisting his big frame round, shaking his head disdainfully at the lot of you, he shouted there was as much chance of Bannigan finally cutting down the Rugby Club sign or Waldo sending Porter the inflatable rubber woman as there was of this one happening, and Joe, quite serious, concentrating hard on the dark twisting road and the guttie well down, fucking right, that sign's coming down the night, shouting to Allie did he still have the bolt-cutters, all of you cracking up, and Waldo shouting that Porter was getting that rubber woman too by the way, he'd seen the very one in a jotter, Lovely Linda, she never said no.

Then the Capri going past you, Joe straight off with the stereo, and he said it was the guys from the pool table, he definitely recognized the guy's bird smirking at him out the back window. And all of you shouting at once, take the bastard Joe, and blow the fucker into the weeds, Joe with the guttie full down, you could see the guy's tail lights getting quickly closer, everybody suddenly quiet in the brief, letting Joe concentrate, the four of you trying to brace yourselves in the back as he slammed it round the sharp turns but still getting flung into one another, one way then back the other, and Joe catching the guy and going for it right before the wee stone bridge, you could tell the guy couldn't believe it, his brake lights coming on just as you started to pull past, and just like that he was gone, blown into the weeds and no arguments about it. But the bridge suddenly right in front of you, and you were going way too fast, you saw Joe fighting with the wheel, pulling it one way then the other, the back end sliding out from under him and he was battling desperately to get it back, and then somehow you were on the tiny narrow bridge, and over it, the brief back under control, and all of you giving it yeeee-haaaa, Waldo and Mack both shouting it was the most fucking amazing piece of driving they ever saw, and Joe, cool as you like to Nate, give us that helmet up big man, out with the targets from the top pocket, the wheel held in one hand as he put them on, and then the helmet put on as well, rally-driver style, the shades and the tinted visor just the thing for his vision on the pitch black road, and Joe with the guttie full down anyway, the music back on and it was the Pistols giving it No Feelings, all of you hooting and cheering, high as kites, and Nate hooting more than anyone, practically ending himself, fucking brilliant Joe, fucking brilliant, you've got the targets, and over and over, you've got the helmet on Joe, you've got the helmet on.

Then back in Kirkie in no time, the dark hills looming behind you as you came down, and Joe saying you could all stay the night at Shiloh, his old man was just after a trip to the Cash and Carry and with a few cases in, he wouldn't miss the odd tin, you gave that a yeee-haaa too, and then all the windows down as you cruised into the main street, and Joe for some reason up with the chant, intae us, intae us, easy, easy, what did it even mean, and all of you now, intae us, intae us, easy, easy, the ones at the windows, Joe himself and Allie and Waldo and even Nate with the clenched fists out, punching the air, and the few scattered souls still around on the pavements looking up at you startled and bewildered as you cruised past, intae us, intae us, easy, easy, you were half way to Shiloh before you finally gave it a bye.

Waiting in the brief for Joe to come back and give the all-clear, King and Kong flying out as soon as he opened the back door, the two of them mental, chasing each other round the big yard, barking and growling, you were glad you were safe in the brief, crammed and uncomfortable as it was, and then you heard the door slamming, Joe struggling to keep hold of the big pile of sleeping bags and blankets, just about making it over to the old rusty caravanette parked in the yard and heaving the stuff in, and all of you tumbling out of the brief then, stretching and trying to get the circulation back in your limbs, you felt your head clear a wee bit in the cold air, the dogs jumping up on you excitedly and Mack loving it of course, playing with them like puppies, you acted as cool as you could, and Joe with not a word about what happened inside, you knew better than to ask when his face was like it was, and change of plan he said, it was a team wade to Drumshants, just lie low in the caravanette and give him a minute till he could sneak out a couple of tins.

Then parked up in the lay-by at Drumshanty, Joe as good as his word and a whole case at your feet on the floor, everybody with a tin going, sat facing each other along the two bottom bunks, everything in soft focus through the thick smoke from the smeegs, Nate and Waldo and Mack all with a crash each already, and the reason Joe wouldn't join you on the bunks, he had the driver's window full down and taking big gulps out his tin, he needed to catch up he said. And taking big breaths too of the cold November air, you could smell the pines yourself even through the blanket of smoke, Waldo asking Mack if it was Steamhammer Hauns he meant, and he said he did, the only time in his life he'd been praying for a handjob to end, there was more chance of dying than coming with the technique she had, and finally the bright idea of asking for a blowjob and stopping it that way, and Nate, for fuck's sake c-balls, that lassie's in the church choir with my old dear, and he said please tell me you didn't just come right out and ask her for a blowjob, and Mack indignant, of course he didn't, and give him some credit, he knew how to put these things, Nate looking at him doubtfully, and Mack, the big guileless coupon on him, I just said get your gums round it.

The tears of laughter running down your face, you looked over and saw Joe crashed out, arm hooked over the windowsill and his head slumped down into the crook of it, you could see his breath blasting out into the cold air with every grunt and snore, and Waldo said his neck was screaming in agony already, but nothing you could do about it, he'd be out for hours knowing Joe, and no point in trying to wake him up, you knew that from experience, he'd be up before any of you in the morning anyway and boasting about how many tins he'd tanned the night. And you were suddenly exhausted yourself, the bev catching up to you at last, and you told them you were crashing too, you stood up and pulled the top bunk out from the side, and you could see they were all set for hours yet, a good three quarters of the case still to be tanned, and you knew the stories would be endless, climbing up and flattening yourself on the bunk, pushing the concertina roof up with your hands for some breathing space, and then you shrugged yourself into the sleeping bag, jeans, jacket and everything, it was a cold night out there. Of course they pulled the roof down on you a couple of times, you knew they would, and probably disappointed if they didn't, but then that was it, maybe they got bored or more likely forgot, and you could hardly blame them for that, the bev to be tanned, and the smeegs to be crashed, and the smoky pine-scented air so full of stories and laughter and good times, it felt like money in the bank somehow to leave them to it.

And you lay there half-listening, the first peace since Gillian was last beside you, and your mind leaving even that with hardly a pang, drifting back instead to the big recess bed in your Grandma's room and kitchen, the adults talking, your mum and your Grandma and your Pop, the ILP and James Maxton, and was the working man worth fighting for, lying there so safe and contented, only half-understanding and that was more than enough, just drifting, and so happy to drift, the words and phrases reaching you and their meanings were in safe hands, nothing for you to do, no need to worry or strive, safe and contented, my fucking ring plan, the tadger's driving on a baldy slick, get your balls out you're on next, you should've seen the johnny I had, there's no way he's riding her, I'm telling you get across the tank, the voices and the laughter, and the peace of it, half-understanding, so safe and contented, and drifting and drifting and drifting.

15

The wee square shopping centre at the top of the hill and Joe spotting the exec parking spot right outside the Steeple, you piled out of the caravanette and then remembered that the shelter was right beside you, the big crowd waiting for the bus, it was mainly women, and what must they have made of you, staggering out one after the other, stinking and disheveled and every one of you in jeans and Wrangler jacket, a few empty tins spilling out as well and clanking down onto the tarmac, you hoovered them up and back in as quickly as you could, and then the whole team of you straight into the boozer for more of the same, barely ten minutes since they opened, you could only hope there was no-one there that knew your mum. Trying to force down a pint of shandy, half and half, and Joe with the shandy too, the rest of them on regular pints except for Waldo, he was swearing by his hangover cure brandy and port as usual, and how he could even stand the fumes from the thing never mind drink it was a total mystery, but anyway you started to feel a wee bit better after a few tentative sips at the shandy, and Joe none the worse for his night out in the open so it seemed, his neck was completely fine he said, and the rest of him too, except that he was fucking hank, wading to the bar to see if he could scare up a couple of pies till the lunches started, you thought you might as well wade up there with him, and hardly even glancing at it really, the telly flickering away behind the bar, a few seconds earlier or later and you'd have missed it altogether.

But still no mistaking what it was, and what it meant, the big depression out in the Atlantic and the calm high pressure at the shore, the swell rolling in right now probably, and if not now it would arrive by tomorrow, and straight into your head the snatches of conversation as you sorted your gear at Duke's garage, the reverential tones at any mention of the north shore, and the whole east coast was dead flat by comparison so they said, the wave up north as heavy as any wave in the world, and if you could ride that you could ride anything. Knowing instantly then that you were going, the need to settle this too, to answer the summons and be quits with it, the debt you owed pushed from your mind for a while but never forgotten, and never would be forgotten, the sea intimating how it was to be honoured, and you were glad it was to be so quick and decisive, you felt strong again, ready to face it when it came to you, and to accept the outcome whatever it was, your goodbyes said quickly now to Joe and then the rest of the team and you must have had something about you, even Mack with just the token protest when you said you'd have to miss tonight, you had something you had to do, looking searchingly at you but he accepted it of course, and you wanted to tell him it was okay, it was out of his hands as much as yours, but you just let him say his piece, he was arranging a midweek fixture at the Vale he said, full turnout required and no excuses accepted, and you said that was fine, you'd see them all there, Joe's voice booming across as you got to the door, where the fuck was the nippy, and how the fuck was he supposed to eat two pies with no nippy.

Sitting your mum and dad down with a cup of tea, the benign curiosity on their faces, and you told them just the way you'd told the team, the short no-nonsense summary of surfing and of Dunallan, and sure enough you saw the relief in their eyes now, all the terrible things you could have been doing, all those times away in the brief, and not that there wasn't interest too, their interest a given in anything you or Louise did, but still mainly it was relief, and funny in a way how Gillian was the only one who'd understood it, how lucky you'd been that it was her you'd chosen to tell first, and the stab of pain from it even still catching you by surprise. And maybe why it took you a moment to see the relief turn to concern, and to register why that was, your own manner too grave and earnest, rattling away about the north shore and how you had to drive up there right away, and almost as if you were guiding them unconsciously to the dark place in your heart, the image of the brief parked undiscovered day after day in some remote lay-by, and they wouldn't even know what happened to you, it was more than you could bear to think about, and why you had to tell them at least where you were going, but still worrying them was the last thing you'd intended, it was just in case was all, cursing yourself for the clumsiness of it, and your mum looking anxiously at you now, tell me it isn't dangerous Andy, you said no of course not, it was just a particular kind of wave they had up there, a really good one, and you wanted to surf it before the swell was gone, the determined effort then to lighten things, laughing and joking with them, and giving them each a casual wee hug for reassurance, you nearly held on too long and blew the whole thing.

Your wetsuit howked out of the big cupboard and flung in the boot with a sleeping bag, and when you turned the key in the ignition the stereo starting up simultaneously with the engine, and Tom Petty blasting out, him and his pals up all night again, it made you smile, but still you turned it off quickly, the need for your mind to be clear of those things, and what would come would come, driving in silence to Duke's for the rest of your gear, and come it did, the north shore breaks, a match for any wave in the world, the hushed reverential tones, and so vivid in your mind the huge slabs of grey granite, the high perfect barrels forming on the flat stone reefs, and a new spot round every bend in the road so they said, each one heavier than the last, and you had to intervene and take charge, the debt to be honoured, and the score to be settled, that was all that was to it and nothing more, and yet you felt your soul quickening, awed and possessed, an effort even to shake yourself loose, but still you did it, the memory of that day at Dunallan still close at hand and all too ready to serve, the loss of hope and things to hope for, and the crushing pain of it was surely not to be borne again, the need to be free of it now, to meet your obligation and to pay your debt, what the sea extended to you that day, and how it ended, the fine thoughts and the high hopes banished, and in their place maybe an easier life at least to come back to, and the thought coming then before you could stop it, maybe no life, and no coming back, and now you really had to intervene, and to take a hold of yourself, there was even less point in thinking about that.

Duke himself sorting through some of his gear when you opened the door of the garage, the surprise and pleasure on his face, and he said it's great to see you Andy, and where had you been these couple of months, you said you'd needed a break and he frowned at that but fair enough he said, and actually you still didn't look so hot now that he looked at you, are you sure you're all right, and you told him aye fine, it was just that you'd been out all night on the bevy, but he said no, it's more than that Andy, you don't seem quite like yourself somehow. An awkward moment then, you tried to think of something to say, and then Duke, hey that was some display you put on for the lassie, and how he'd been out walking his dog and saw you, the turns off the lip and the good deep snaps, you were a natural and no mistake, he never saw anyone come so far in so short a time, though no wonder in a way, he never saw anyone work so hard either, and he said the lassie seemed to be enjoying it too, was it your girlfriend, and even now it took you all your strength, you said ex-girlfriend, and he said ach that's too bad Andy, she seemed nice, and you said aye, she was nice.

The awkward silence again, and you saw Duke groping for a way to break it, you loved him for that, and he said what about the two of you grabbing a pint, he feared you'd had a wasted journey otherwise, there was nothing round these parts the day but close-outs, and it was the guys up north that had the swell, lucky bastards that they were, a few years younger and he might have had a drive up there himself, and you took your chance, the need to tell Duke eerily like the need to tell your mum and dad, you said actually that was where you were headed, you were only swinging by to pick up your board, and cursing at the wee silly laugh following the words out of your mouth, you saw Duke notice it, and the frown come back on his face, and you braced yourself, you knew exactly what was coming. Sure enough, the frown deepening on his tough weather-beaten coupon, and he didn't fuck about, you'd have been shocked if he did, he said you don't know what you're saying son, you maybe think you do but you don't, and he said did you even know it was hard-core granite on the bottom of those reefs up there, and not a heavier wave in the whole world, one single wipeout could kill you for God's sake, and when you tried to argue, and you could feel the huge riddie you had, Duke holding up a placatory hand, and a softer tone now, just give it another season Andy, that's all I'm saying, the way you're going you'll be ready then I promise, and his eyes almost pleading with you, he said why don't we call it a deal, this time next year and I'll drive you up there myself if you like, holding out his hand to you right there in the garage, and all the surfing gear piled around you on all sides, his eyes still fixed on yours, and the pleading in his voice now too, you're just not ready Andy, you're just not ready son.

Looking down at your feet, you felt your coupon burning hot, and what could you say, there was nothing to say, you lifted your head up at last and looked miserably back at him, the concern in his eyes that was just like anger, and then right as you looked the fire of it gone, and the understanding there in its place, the same expression you'd seen that very first day you met him, and the words in your head as clear now as then, you just want to get out there, don't you Andy, giving a big sigh now, okay, fair enough, if that's how it is then that's how it is, and you saw a new thought come into his head and register on his face, he said wait there Andy son, and bouncing out the side-door before you could even ask him why or what for, not that you would have anyway, your heart full from the look he'd given you, you watched out of the wee back window as he louped up the path of the long narrow garden and into the house, the energy radiating off him, the gait of a man half his age, and nothing for it but to sit back down on your board and wait.

A full ten minutes till the garage door opened again, I've a couple of things for you Andy, holding out the brand-new wetsuit to you, and it was top grade neoprene he said, five-three thickness, he'd been going to wait till the stuff you had was paid off, and the winters here never so bad anyway, but you'd need it for sure on the north shore, brass-monkey time up there, and that was the least of it, suicide to go anywhere near those reefs without your best armour on, you could take it from him. Holding up his hand again when you tried to thank him, and to pay him something on account, ach I ken you're good for it son, we'll work it out when you come back, and then the sly grin, holding the door open with his foot, and reaching round to the outside wall, I said a couple of things did I not, your breath near taken away when you saw it, the beautiful new board, streamlined and smooth and bright, the deep burnished gold of it, and the dark red lightning bolt imprinted on the deck, standing it up beside you so you could see properly the length of it, the quiet pride of him when he saw the joy it gave you, and when you said it was definitely shorter than the one you had, was it six and a half, smiling proudly too, not bad not bad, it was six-eight actually, and ten pounds, the rounded pintail and the single fin just the job for what you'd be facing up there, and the fire back in his eyes then as he looked at you, we'll get you by that north shore yet Andy son.

Coming out to help you tie the board onto the brief, the new wetsuit tucked away in the boot, and he said be sure and stop by on your way back down the road tomorrow, you said you would, and he looked you hard in the eye again, I mean it Andy, it doesn't matter how late it is, I'm always up till yon time anyway, his hand firm on your shoulder, and you told him again that you would for sure, the need suddenly to be away and on the road, you got the guttie down the moment you turned the corner, and tuning the radio with one hand as you drove, you didn't want music but just voices only, out of range for Radio Clyde but you found Radio Scotland and that was fine, the plummy studio accents and feeling good now, and at peace again, Duke and his kind concerned eyes, the beautiful gold board tied securely on the roof and the thick suit of rubber armour in the boot, hugging your mum and dad, and how many times had they hugged you over the years, the warmth and the comfort of it, and hurtling around in the Campsie Hills, the corners taken on two wheels in the pitch black night, and practically in Lennoxtown before the helmet even came off, intae us, intae us, easy, easy, you were all the way onto the A9 when you finally came to and listened to what the plummy voices were saying.

The events of the week under discussion in the studio, and all of them with their opinions on Foot becoming the new Labour leader, a surprise really, everyone expected Healey to win, the Left were jubilant so they said, and the clip of Tony Benn, how pleased he was, and what a great day for the Party, and Gillian would be pleased too you supposed though you wondered what had changed, and how sure she'd been on the phone that it would be Benn himself would be going for it, one more reason why it wasn't for you, and the same with your mum and the union, the deals and the shifts and the turns, you never understood any of it, but still good luck to them, and maybe Gillian was right even and they really were getting somewhere at last. And sure enough, story after story then on how badly Thatcher was doing, and all the plummy voices in agreement, unemployment up another half million, the unions taking a maddie over the pay limits she set, and the clip of the shop steward from Linwood, the bastards were trying to close the place down he said, the firemen set to strike, and Heath and MacMillan and the CBI guy all wading in too, how the ones really suffering were the business community, all of them in the studio agreeing with that too, how long could she last the way it was going, and then you couldn't help but smile, the clip of Joe Gormley at some conference in London, and there was going to be anarchy he said, anarchy in the streets, and most likely the streets of Glasgow according to Joe, you said it out loud to yourself, right there cruising along in the brief, must be about time for us to smash the fucking state, and big Graham probably snorting into his Buckie, he'd no time for Gormley, or for Foot or Benn either come to that, but maybe pleased a wee bit all the same for the mention.

Then the smile off your face, the next story was the hunger strike at Long Kesh, the Maze they called it, and the clip of Thatcher, the awful voice she had, and what it revealed, haughty and grating and superior, devoid of kindness, no humanity in it even, and there would be no concessions to terrorism she said. Seeing her so clearly then, the headmistress at some posh school and one of the kids up to some childish jape, the sullen insolent face of him, starving himself to death, and he was just doing it for the attention, ignore him and he'll stop his foolishness soon enough, your dad was surely right, how long would she last if she had to spend one day in the H-Blocks, and how long would any of them last, the whole thing would be settled the minute they had to miss their breakfast. The image of Gillian outside the GFT, the tears of anger you thought and no she said, it was shame, and when they decided it was a war you were just supposed to go along, Earl Haig the Butcher of the Somme, thousands of men slaughtered for no reason, just a game to him, a chestful of medals and a charity named after him, and when they decided it was terrorism you had to go along with that too, think of the innocent victims, and fuck all they cared about the victims, the same men and women and children they killed in every war and never gave a fuck, the guys that dropped the bombs on Hiroshima and Nagasaki, the foulest crime imaginable, and medals and parades for them too, starving yourself to death for the right to wear your own clothes, and to talk to your mates, and what the fuck did she know of any of it, what did any of the fuckers know, the rage and despair, and the loss of hope, the loss of hope and things to hope for.

The plummy voices in the studio, and all in agreement now with Thatcher of course, what else would you expect, the cosy club of it, and proving you all had the right values whatever else you disagreed about, starving yourself to death not to be tolerated, a firm line needed against rage and despair, you were reaching to turn it off, and then the clip of Foot, the Government could rely on the full support of the Opposition, we can make no concessions to terrorism, and now you did turn it off, the tears in your eyes, and what were they even for, it was Gillian that believed in it and not you, you'd tried to tell her, and to stop her, the Party and the people and Foot and Benn, marching and campaigning, giving them all of yourself, the badges gone in two seconds, and Troops Out Now, all of it as useless as tears, the anger and the shame, we're the heart of darkness Andy, the heart of darkness, driving in silence again, it was all you wanted, the beautiful gold board on the roof, and your armour in the boot, the dark road ahead, and in your mind so clear the huge barreling waves and the hard grey granite of the north shore.

16

First light in the bay, looking out the back window at the empty road, not a single car to be seen and were they Wee Frees up here, maybe you weren't even supposed to be stirring on the Sabbath, but then there'd been none last night either, and one of the reasons you turned down here, the thunder of the waves the loudest you'd heard on the whole north shore, past Thurso and past Brims Ness, and driving further and further west along the coast in the thick winter darkness, the sea was telling you where it was to be done, listening to the fearsome sounds echoing off the hills behind, and this was the place, you were sure of that, down the single track and parked right on the very edge of the bay, the terrible grandeur of it haunting your dreams, stretching now and rubbing your aching limbs, sleeping bag unzipped, and the cold grey light, you dared yourself to look out the front window and face the source of the extraordinary sound.

Then watching and watching for the longest time, the first time ever you were scared of the sea, so grim and vengeful it seemed, and Duke's voice in your head, you're just not ready Andy, standing at the top of the big chute, the bitter wind whistling in your ears, and the big kids had to pass you down through the rails and into his arms, your Pop so silent and angry, the only time ever and you knew fine well why, there was never a thing he'd shirked in his life, and yet so proud of you still, the postcard in his fine neat hand, and your mum crying, she was crying for her children she said, the crash of thunder as the wall of water came swelling out of the deep and smashed into the shallow granite reef, jacking up and sectioning all along the length of it, the huge hollow barrels and the exploding white spray, the bottom of the wave became the top in the very moment you watched, so grand and solemn and vengeful, and you said I promise I'll go down it Pop, the bond to be honoured and the debt repaid, and your promise spoken aloud, one way or another you would be free and clear of it this day.

Untying your board from the roof, your movements were quick and efficient now, a good coat of wax on the deck, and your shiny new armour on, running strongly on the clean white sand, and flat onto your board, all your momentum checked almost at once in the freezing cold of it, and the ice-cream headache almost instantaneous too, paddling out and trying to find the channel, and you couldn't find it, you couldn't tell if it was the headache or the spray or the cold, or maybe there really was a mist coming down, but so hard to see, and as if nothing else could withstand the thunderous energy of the waves, dare to assert its own existence in the face of such daunting force and power. A miracle too if you could even find the lineup, but you kept the nose pointing out to sea and paddling even harder now, the clean-up set almost on you before you saw it, and you knew at once that you were caught inside and that you weren't going to make it, but your board so streamlined and swift and light, you climbed somehow over the first mountainous face with not an inch to spare, and paddling then with everything you had, the second wave even bigger than the first, up and up on the face, closer to making it than you would have believed was possible, but still the sickening inevitability, you weren't going to make it, you were caught, the biggest wave you'd ever come close to, and no time even to roll off your board and try to dive through the solid grey wall of it, you and your board picked up already, you saw your feet come up over your head, and then you were being sucked backwards, the sheer naked terror of it, a split second as you saw your beautiful board shoot up into the air, and then the sea swallowed you, and there was nothing but the terror and the chaos.

Worked and thrashed and beaten, tumbling and tumbling, forwards then backwards and then forwards again, twisting in every possible direction, you didn't know which way was up or down, right or left, tumbling and tumbling, and worked now along the bottom of the reef, every part of your body beaten against the rocks, all you could do was endure it and hope for it to end, and then the sudden moment of relative calm, you took a guess at the direction for the surface and kicked hard, and almost instantly you were breaking the surface and gulping down air, the light that had seemed so grey seeming so bright now, and like a dream almost, I can make it, I'm going to survive. Seeing it then, the next wave in the set, and you saw too that you were still in the impact zone, the wave another monster and driving you straight back down, and over and over, thrashed and worked on the reef, and then falling, the strangest sensation of all, a waterfall under water, down and down, the dull awareness of what was causing it, your body dragged off the shallow reef by the current and into the deep water, and no way to know how deep it might be, tumbling and tumbling, falling and falling.

And though you knew it could only be a few seconds it felt like a million years, and a million thoughts in your head at once, the solemn way they passed the joint around, whose crash is it for the smeegs, the smug pompous face of him as he handed you your pint, the meanings safe and secure somewhere, the sea understood it you knew, the debt paid and your obligations honoured, I promise I'll go down it Pop, his face cut and bleeding, and still none of them helped him, taking all that he had but they wouldn't help him, we're the heart of darkness Andy, drifting and drifting, and blissful now, detached from it all, the dark invisible workmanship drawing all the thoughts inexorably into one thought, and you waited to see what it would be, the mild and blissful curiosity of it, the pressure in your ears, and darker and darker, deeper and deeper, so deep you can't get under it, so wide you can't get around it, a tired old horse and a man bent over a hand-held plough, you knew it from somewhere, time to smash the fucking state, you knew that from somewhere too, smash the fucking state, the sea understood it, the meaning safe and secure, drifting and drifting and drifting.

Then the mood of the water changing in a heartbeat, and you were being pushed up, and so quickly up, the pain in your ears so intense and sharp, you saw the tumult still above you, and then you broke the surface again, shooting up like your board, like a ball held under water and suddenly released, and now you were outside the break, the huge wave taking hold of you but not driving you down, holding you instead, and carrying you, the incredible speed of it, and the clean white sand already so close, you could see the beach and the hills looming up towards you, and then you were touching the sand, rolling and flopping like a landed fish, and coughing and retching, though there was little or nothing you knew in your stomach, gobbing the foul-tasting stuff onto the pristine sand, and it was bile you supposed, the tide would come soon and wash it away.

Lying flat on your back, looking at the sky and laughing from the joy of it, the joy of being alive, and how absurd it seemed already, you hardly knew what you'd been thinking, debts and repayments and the settling of scores, as if the sea would ever trouble itself with such trifling capers, the busy dance of things that pass away, and the feeling so strong again now, the power you'd learned to revere, the fervent desire for something loftier, it was the bond and nothing less that had called you here. The thoughts that came to you in the deep dark water, lying laughing now on the clean white sand, time to smash the fucking state, and Gillian's old man, the smug pompous coupon of him, Earl Haig, the Butcher of the Somme, and Thatcher and Foot, every one of them just as absurd here, the huge barreling waves still crashing on the granite reef, and the clean white sand, the whole of it breathing with inward meaning, exalted by reason, sanctified by truth.

Then the meaning of it drifting gently to the front of your mind, and as if it had been there always and just waiting for you to find it, his face cut and bleeding, and people were scared to get involved he said, but he wasn't scared, they wouldn't help him and still he wasn't scared, and refusing to change, seeing it so clearly at last, the fervent desire for something loftier, the need to connect to others, and to share yourself, the instinct in him that was as strong as hope, they wouldn't do it for you Sam, and it wasn't the point, you saw it now, his own soul the point and his own humanity, even the people couldn't take it from him. It was what they hated, the cosy wee club of them, Earl Haig and Thatcher, and Foot trying to join, starving yourself to death for the right to talk to your mates, and they wouldn't help you, a strong line to be taken, their own humanity long gone, the things they blazoned with the pompous names of power and action, his soul was free of it, the instinct he had inside him, and it was inside everyone surely, inside them somewhere, feeling it so strong at last in yourself, a living voice in your soul, and not to be withstood now, they wouldn't do it for you, and it wasn't the point, the strength and consolation of it, and the image suddenly of Duke's kind compassionate eyes, you're not ready Andy, you're not quite yourself, lying and laughing on the beautiful white sand, he was right you knew, you weren't yourself then, and now as fully yourself as you'd ever been, sitting up to see as well as hear, the huge barrels thundering on the shallow reef, and you were as ready as anyone could ever be.

The pale winter sun low in the sky and the mist gone if there had even been one, you still didn't know, your board retrieved and the channel found easily, paddling out and into the lineup, and making yourself act before you could think, the towering wall of water, the astonishing speed of it, and jacking up higher and higher as you dropped in, somehow you caught it, and plunging down the face, just trying to survive, no chance you could make the bottom turn, you thrust an arm full into the icy torrent of it, the hope of stalling for even a split-second, and instantly you could feel it, the pervading grace and exalted mood, and as if time itself felt it, your board turned frontside and stalled on the face, the inside rail hard into the thundering wave, and the wave so generous, suspending time, holding you there on the steep glassy wall while the roaring curl of it caught you, and passed you, the barrel cascading over your head, and in a heartbeat you were inside the tube, encased completely in the roaring thunderous energy of it, frontside to the deep dark wall, and the white water surging and exploding above and behind you, your board so fast and so smooth inside the wave, one second and two, and you felt the exuberant whoosh of spray shoot up the barrel towards you, easing quickly then onto your front foot, eyes watchful and holding your line, arm pointed out at the unbroken face, and surging forward as the barrel closed out behind, the wave in front sectioning too now, you took the lowest line you could, gliding into the wide bottom turn, and skirting the foaming white water so smoothly, your soul overflowing, your heart wide open, and you couldn't help yourself, the yeee-haaa worthy of Bo Duke himself, you hardly even winced at the incongruous echo of it from the stately hills looming so high over the bay.

Ready to kick out and paddle back to the beach, hardly believing the words yourself as they formed in your head, riding inside the barrel at the north shore, and yet already other words coming too, this is who I am and this is what I do, may you never stop looking for that perfect wave, and at the edge of your vision the fresh hollow section forming ahead, and as if the sea was willing you on now, there was more of this yet, carving easily past the last of the white water, then crouching down, willing your board to catch up to it, the thoughts crowding into your head, stopping at Duke's on the road home, it wouldn't even be that late, hugging your mum and dad, and you'd hold on for as long as you wanted, the midweek fixture with the team, and maybe you would phone Karen Clarke, and as if you'd have any peace from Mack till you did, trimming a good bit up the face and speeding so fast again into the tube, hand on the wave to stall yourself, weight on your back foot, and you felt the lip come crashing over you, the high clean thundering barrel so magnanimous, and the words again in your head, except that they weren't words any more, or thoughts even, just images in a dream that began somewhere in your mind and then flowed along your soul, our destiny, our nature and our home is with infinitude, and only there, with hope it is, hope that can never die, in the very heart now of the wave, the smooth glassy wall and the white water pulsing and cascading and exploding all round you, wholly inside the barrel, the tumult and the peace of it, life's mysterious weight of pain and fear, the pain of connection, and losing the ones you loved, and so grateful for it now, the pain that you'd always have, the pride that it was part of you, the beautiful gold of your board, and the flash of red, speeding so smoothly inside the huge hollow wave, the white and grey and streaks of yellow and blue, looking all round you and remembering, the sky and the pale winter sun through the high cascading glass wall, the day just beginning, effort and expectation, and desire, and something evermore about to be.

Printed in Great Britain
by Amazon

59269203R00126